BROTHER'S RUIN

INDUSTRIAL MAGIC, BOOK 1

EMMA NEWMAN

A TOM DOHERTY ASSOCIATES BOOK

NEW YORK

This is a work of fiction. All of the characters, organizations, and events portrayed in this novella are either products of the author's imagination or are used fictitiously.

For Tim Knight,
a wonderful man
who knows the value of a good brother

Brother's Ruin

Chapter 1

CHARLOTTE GUIDED HER BROTHER to the right position on the pavement, ignoring the glares from other Londoners as they stopped the flow of people hurrying about their business. Soon she and Benjamin became like a little rock in the stream of people, moved around with ease now they were predictably still.

"May I open my eyes yet?" Ben asked.

"No."

She could feel his arm trembling. Anyone else and she would have assumed it was the cold; the bitter November wind had teeth today. It was the furthest Ben had walked in weeks, and she feared she'd taken him too far from home. His lips were pale beneath his brown moustache, his cheeks still rather gaunt. She would hail a hansom cab to take them home. There were plenty clattering up and down the cobbles behind them.

She lined him up in front of the display, leaving her hands wrapped around his arm to steady him. "Now you can open them."

He blinked at the sight of the shop window, a slight

frown creasing his brow as he took in what was displayed on the other side of the glass. "Charlie, is that . . . ?"

She beamed. "Yes!"

"I'd recognise your work anywhere!"

"Shush," she whispered, glancing at the people walking past them. None of them seemed to have heard him.

"And you did all of the illustrations?"

"Every single one. It took months. It's already in its third printing and it's only been on sale for a week." She didn't mention that she had walked to this very shop every day to admire the display. There were several copies positioned over a luxurious pile of green velvet, artfully arranged to hide the boxes positioned underneath to give the display several platforms for the books. Three copies were clipped open, to show different examples of her artwork. One of them was the illustration she was most proud of: a medieval knight kneeling at his true love's tomb. The collection's title, *Love, Death and Other Magicks,* was displayed on a large board behind the books, as if the embossed covers were not sufficient, with *A collection of poetry by Thackery Brown, illustrated by Charles Baker* written underneath in elegant copperplate. "The sales are because of the poetry, of course, not my small contribution. It really is the best collection I've ever read."

Ben looked down at her, his left eyebrow spiked upwards. "Darling, the collection is exquisite and successful because of your *substantial* contribution. Your illustrations do far more to form the first impression than anything else." He rested his hand over hers and pressed it against his arm. "I am so proud of you. And so very grateful."

Charlotte felt the heat in her cheeks and looked away. "It's nothing."

She felt his kiss on the top of her head. "You deserve recognition. I'm not talking about everything you've done for me. I mean as an artist. You're so talented."

Her heart flipped unpleasantly at the thought of anyone else other than her brother and her agent knowing about her secret career. Not even George, her fiancé, knew about it. "I earn more under a male pseudonym, you know that."

Ben waved a hand at the display. "This collection is the talk of London. I heard that the Royal Society of Esoteric Arts ordered fifty copies for their library, and there are rumours that the Queen herself has been seen with it. If you revealed your identity as the illustrator, then . . ."

"Don't be silly, Ben. I need the money—we need it! My agent can only command such high fees when the publishers think I'm a man."

"But you're not listening to me, dear heart. If people knew you were the one who illustrated this collection, you wouldn't be disadvantaged by your sex. Times are changing! The Royal Society has proven that women are just as able as men. They—"

Charlotte pulled away, looking for a cab. "It's one rule for the magi, another for everyone else."

"Magus Magda Ravensthorpe has a female accountant. I read it in the *Times* only this morning! Even for the magi, she's one of the wealthiest people in the Empire. She's making a statement. Perhaps you could do the same in the arts."

"I'm not wealthy enough to make a statement." Why were there no cabs now she needed one?

"But you're talented enough. I've a good mind to write to the *Times* and tell them who Charles Baker really is. It's in the public interest!"

She scowled at him. "You'll do no such thing, Benjamin Gunn. I would never forgive you. And if my wishes are not enough to dissuade you, consider our parents. Mother would be appalled that all those times she thinks I've been tutoring young ladies have actually been spent drawing pictures, and Father would be embarrassed. I already earn twice as much as him per commission and my agent believes that will only increase thanks to *Other Magicks*. I couldn't bear it if he felt upstaged by his own daughter."

Ben shook his head. "They would be proud. They'd be

relieved! At least one of their children is capable of making something of their life!"

She clasped his hand, gripping it tight. "You are perfectly capable, too! You've just met a bump in the road, that's all."

The fear in his eyes didn't need to be voiced. She tried to look confident, to look certain that he would be able to complete his studies, all the while desperately hoping he couldn't see her doubts. She was just about to say something when the clang of a bell cut through the noise of the street and made her gut cramp with terror.

"Let's cut through to Bond Street," she said, doing all she could to hide the panic from her voice. "There must be cabs there."

But Ben was craning his neck, using his height to peer over the heads of the women on the street and even some of the top hats. "I think that's an Enforcer's bell."

But how could they have found out what she was? She'd been so careful. "You look pale and I've brought you too far, too soon." Charlotte pulled his hand. "Time to go home."

"Gosh! It *is* the Enforcers! They're heading this way! How splendid! I've always wanted to see *the* gauntlet. Charlie, stop pulling! Don't you want to see it, too?"

"No. It isn't any of our business." Charlotte feared her heart was going to punch its way through the bones of her corset if she didn't get away. The bell's mournful clang reverberated through the street, bouncing off the stone of the buildings until it sounded like it was coming from all directions at once. Her lips started to tingle and it felt like the blood in her veins was somehow seeping through the soles of her feet, into the pavement. Had someone reported her? Why? She never did anything to give anyone cause to summon the Enforcers.

Ben wrested his arm from her grip and she staggered away, taking a moment to right herself. She wanted to run, but she couldn't leave her brother, so frail, to make it back home without her. No doubt he'd forgotten his coin purse, and besides, he was dreadful at summoning cabs. If it hadn't been for the prospect of a dramatic spectacle, she was sure he would be swaying by now. But above any concern for his health was the simple selfish fact that she didn't want him to see her being dragged off, weeping and screaming.

She backed away as the dark shape of the horseless carriage came into view, a sliver of black glimpsed between the shoulders of the gathering crowd. It was large and, like any normal Clarence carriage, fully enclosed with the capacity to carry several passengers at once. But unlike a Clarence, there were no horses pulling it. A driver sat at the front as usual, but he was masked, dressed in black and moving the wheels with his esoteric knowledge. Only the fact his hand was held out in front of him, holding a Focus, suggested he was involved in driving the vehicle at all. Whatever the Focus was, it was too small to be seen, cupped as it was in the magus's hand.

Charlotte's legs almost gave out from under her at the sight of the driver's mask. It was dark red, featureless with only holes for the eyes, covering the entire face and positioned over a black veil so not even any hair or skin on the neck could be seen. Every couple of seconds, he—or she, perhaps—clanged the bell that hung from a hook at the side of the carriage, there to warn pedestrians of its approach in lieu of the clattering of horses' hooves.

The carriage was slowing. They must have spotted her. Ben forgotten in her blind panic, Charlotte span around and tried to make a dash for the nearby cut through to Bond Street, but too many bystanders had gathered behind her. She bounced off a portly gentleman in a half-caped coat who scowled at her and didn't move an inch. Behind her, the carriage was drawing to a stop and she could barely breathe. The man grabbed her by the shoulders and just as she was about to berate him for his rudeness, she realised he thought she was fainting. "My wife has some smelling salts!" he said, the words puffing over her face with breath that smelt of liver and onions. Her stomach heaved as the doors of the carriage opened mere yards away from her.

"Charlotte, are you quite well?" Ben was at her side, gathering her away from the well-meaning man as his wife rummaged in her reticule.

"Tell Mother and Father I'm sorry," she whispered as the sound of boots landing on the cobbles behind her made her shiver violently.

"What was that?" Ben leaned closer but she hadn't the breath to speak again.

Charlotte closed her eyes, waiting for the moment they dragged her from her brother's arms. She should have given herself up. She should have thought of her parents, how submitting herself for testing would have been so much better for them, for Ben, too. She could have solved their financial woes more honestly, could have lived without fear all this time. But no. She was too selfish for that. She'd always felt her love for her fiancé was something beautiful, that wanting to be his wife and make him happy was a far more noble pursuit than magic. Now she understood the depth of her cowardice.

"It's someone in the bakery!" Ben said, and Charlotte listened to the stomp of the boots pass her completely. Stunned, she turned back around to see the Enforcers streaming towards the bakery on the opposite side of the street. "And there's the gauntlet!" Ben whispered to her, wrapping his arms tightly around her so they could lean against each other as they watched, both trembling for very different reasons.

The gauntlet was being carried on a bright blue velvet cushion by someone masked and veiled like the rest. Whoever the bearer was, Charlotte assumed he was a man, judging by the height and broad shoulders. The polished steel glinted in the winter sunshine and they were so close that Charlotte could see the intricate etching that decorated it.

"That's the one the Queen granted to the Royal Society when it was created," Ben whispered in her ear.

"I know," she whispered back.

"The other of the pair is held at the Tower of London," he continued.

"I know."

"It symbolises how the power of the Royal Society can only be fully effective . . ."

Charlotte sighed and elbowed him gently to make him look at her. ". . . when used in concert with the Crown. I know, Ben." She also knew how powerful that symbol was. The Royal Society and the Crown had never needed to unite for military action on English soil, but they had in the far-flung reaches of the Empire, to extend Her Majesty's power across the globe. The Royal Society was eager to demonstrate loyalty and put to bed any rumours that its fellows coveted rulership of the Empire. No matter how many times the tabloids speculated about the power struggle between the nobility and the magi, there was certainly no sign of treason yet.

Ben gave her his best lopsided smile. "Sorry, Charlie. I forget you take much more of an interest in these things than Mother does."

The bearer went to the bakery's door across the street, the other magi fanned out in a semicircle behind him. Three customers leaving the shop with their warm loaves paused briefly on the threshold and then scurried away, clutching their purchases to their chests. On the other side of the line of magi, people who had clearly been about to enter the shop changed their minds. Soon it was empty, save for the baker and one other inside who Charlotte couldn't see.

"It must be the baker's son," Ben said. "He's still in there."

There was a movement inside as someone came from behind the counter and Charlotte listened to the bolts on the door being slid shut. She bit her lip, feeling so guilty being merely a bystander when someone's life was about to be changed forever.

"That was a mistake," Ben said. "Locking them out will only make it worse."

"They're frightened," Charlotte said.

"Cowardly," Ben replied. "Better to face up to it. These reports aren't made lightly. There must be some truth in it."

One of the magi stepped forwards, passing the gauntlet bearer to rap on the door. A formality. Everyone on the street knew it wasn't going to be opened, but the gesture had to be made first. The magus waited a few moments and then returned to the semicircle.

A murmur passed through the crowd, a palpable excitement building. Charlotte wanted to be anywhere but here, surrounded by people feeling so fortunate to have been in the right place at the right time to see an actual arrest. It was nothing but a bit of drama to them, something to talk about in the pub or over dinner, to make other people listen. How could Ben even think of making her career as an illustrator into a similar thing? The scandal of a woman earning as much as a man in the arts would be the same fodder for conversational cattle.

Ben's hold tightened as the gauntlet bearer stepped forwards, making the faint noise of the crowd sink away to silence.

"We have requested entry and it has been refused," the bearer said, his voice a deep, rich baritone.

"We have witnessed it," said the magi in concert with both male and female voices.

"We have knowledge of a threat to the Crown and to the safety of the public. It is our duty to act."

"We will witness it."

The bearer took another step forwards and raised his gloved hand. The gauntlet rose from the cushion, making the thrilled crowd gasp in awe. With his other hand, the magus passed the now superfluous cushion to his nearest colleague, his attention never leaving the gauntlet hovering in the air in front of him.

From where they were watching, Charlotte could only see that and the corresponding movement of the magus's hand. If the magus was doing anything else, she couldn't see it, nor the Focus he was presumably using.

Charlotte felt a pull in her chest, a need to get closer, and quickly suppressed it. She looked away, preferring to study the mutton chops on a man's face nearby than be tempted towards something rash.

A loud thud and the breaking of glass drew her attention back to the bakery. The gauntlet was drawing back from the door and then was propelled towards it again with enough force to splinter the wood around the lock. The small pane of glass in the top of the door was already broken. The door swung open on the third strike.

The gauntlet and the magus who controlled it moved into the bakery, with his colleagues closing in around the doorway.

The crowd shuffled forwards as the magi advanced and Charlotte was pushed ahead with them. Ben kept his arms around her, knowing she wasn't fond of crowds and probably holding himself up in the process. There were screams and pleading and Charlotte felt tears prick in her eyes at the sound of a mother's distress. Would that be her mother one day?

"Give him up!" a man in the crowd shouted, and others jeered their agreement.

"I always thought he was an odd one," said a woman behind them.

"He isn't odd, just thick," said a jowly faced man. "Too thick to be a magus."

"Hiding his light under a bushel, I reckon," said the woman. "The mother probably put him up to it. Silly old tart. She could have been rich!"

"Maybe she didn't want her son to be taken away," Charlotte said, rounding on them. "Maybe she just wants her son to have a normal life."

The woman, whose cheeks were a lurid red, pursed her lips. "A normal life? What you on about? Who wouldn't want to be rich?"

"But—"

"That selfish woman was holding him back," the woman went on. "I hope they hang her."

"That's rather harsh!" Ben said, and the woman narrowed her eyes at him.

"I think it's treason, and so do lots of others. I 'eard they're talking about it in Parliament. She's been denyin' the Crown and them magi what's rightfully theirs. Not right, that."

"What if the son didn't want to go?" Charlotte asked.

"It's the mother's fault." The woman pointed towards the bakery and the magi who had already started heading to the horseless carriage. The bearer was backing out onto the street and not far behind him the baker's son was being dragged by the gauntlet as if it were being worn by an invisible giant. The boy, a slip of a lad in his mid-teens, was pale faced and obviously trying not to cry as his mother tugged at his free arm until they were all out on the street.

When the carriage door was opened ahead of him, the sight of the dark interior made the boy struggle, too, only fuelling his mother's distress.

"He isn't one of you!" she sobbed. "He's a baker's boy, that's all!"

"He will be tested," one of the magi said. Her voice was firm but not without sympathy. "If he is found to be a Latent, you'll be brought before a magistrate for trial." She held out a scroll tied with red ribbon and sealed with wax. "Take this and let your son go, or it will be all the worse for the two of you."

"You brought it on yerself!" called out the red-faced woman who had made Charlotte feel ill.

"You shut your mouth!" the baker shouted back. "You

don't know nothing about us!"

"Take it and let your son go," the magus said again. "Do this, and I will see him safe," she added.

Charlotte didn't believe her, but it was enough to take the last of the mother's fight out of her. She released her son's arm and sagged. The magus rested a hand on her shoulder and put the scroll into her shaking hands.

"Ma! Ma!" the boy had time to shout before he was bundled inside. The rest of the magi entered the carriage, along with the bearer. The magus who had delivered the scroll climbed up onto the front to drive it away.

Drama over, the crowd drifted apart. Charlotte tried to shut out the judgemental comments and snide remarks directed at the baker and found it impossible. "Haven't you seen enough?" she said to a cluster of people who stared openly at the baker's distress. "Surely there are other tragedies for you to judge elsewhere?"

"Charlie," Ben said gently, but she was angry now.

"Well?" She shrugged his embrace off. "Or is watching a mother crying in the street of the upmost importance to you?"

The group finally felt enough shame to leave, but not without a few comments aimed in her direction about rude young women.

The baker was still standing there, staring at the end of the street where the carriage had last been seen, tears rolling down her cheeks. Charlotte went over to her, ignoring the tuts and the way the stragglers were turning their backs on the poor woman. She gently rested a hand on the woman's arm. "Perhaps it would be best to go inside and sit down? I can make you a cup of tea, if you wish?"

The baker blinked at Charlotte as if she was an apparition and didn't trust her eyes. "My boy," she whispered.

"I know. I'm so sorry," Charlotte said, steering the woman back towards the bakery gently. "Do you have any family I can send for?"

"He was it."

"A friend, perhaps?"

"Not now this has happened."

Charlotte guided her through the door and fetched a chair from the back room as the woman stood ghostlike in her own shop. Once the baker was seated, Charlotte grabbed a dustpan and brush she'd spotted behind the counter and began sweeping up the broken glass. "You'll need a locksmith for your door. I think there's one in the next street along."

The baker broke down, her whole body heaving with each sob. Charlotte set the dustpan and brush down and knelt beside the baker, feeling horribly impotent as she rested a hand on the woman's shoulder.

"Charlie?" Her brother's voice at the doorway made

her look up. The sight of his dreadfully pale face startled her into standing again. "Could you possibly find a cab?"

"Of course, darling." She looked back at the baker. "I'm so sorry. I need to get my brother home. He's been unwell and he needs to rest." The baker didn't acknowledge her. Charlotte moved to the doorway. "I will call by tomorrow, if I can. Please do try to get some help with the door."

"Charlie," her brother said again and she rushed to his side, wrapping one of his arms over her shoulder to help him back onto the street.

"Sorry, darling. Let's get you home."

He kissed the top of her head. "Dear Charlie Bean, always the one to help the least deserving."

"That's not true," she said as she steered him towards Bond Street. "I always help you and no one could deserve that more."

They kept up the gentle banter as they walked but she couldn't pull her mind from the bakery. She needed no further reminder that she was a criminal and a coward, and yet there it was, played out in front of her. How long could she keep her latent magic hidden before she brought that same grief to her own family's door?

Chapter 2

BY THE TIME the hansom cab was pulling into their street, Ben's lips were a disturbing grey colour and Charlotte felt exhausted. It was as if the panic caused by the arrival of the Enforcers had made everything inside her surge like in a spring tide. Now it had all ebbed away, leaving nothing but a churned-up shore and driftwood. *All is well,* she kept telling herself. *No one suspects a thing.* She just had to be careful for two or three more years, until she was a happily married woman in her early twenties and such an unlikely candidate for being a rogue magus that no one would pay her any attention at all.

Charlotte closed her eyes, enjoying the last moments of rest before the cab came to a stop. She imagined her and George, living in one of the little terraced houses just a few streets away, making a life together. He a fully qualified registrar, she an illustrator. She frowned to herself. When should she confess her secret career to her fiancé? The right moment hadn't yet presented itself. He was such a ... sensible man, she wasn't sure he would take the news well. It felt dishonest to keep it from him before they married, but what if he broke their engagement at the news? Perhaps it was better to just carry on as she had for the past two years, working in secret. He knew she was a keen artist, as did her parents. Did he really need to know she had an income of her own?

"'Ere we are then," called the cab driver.

She paid him through the hatch behind her and he released the lock on the carriage doors. It was only when she'd helped Ben down the steps that she realised a man was on their doorstep.

As soon as Charlotte saw him, she instinctively looked away. There was something about the way he peered at them from beneath the brim of a rather tatty bowler hat that made her shudder. He wore a long coat that was expensive but poorly cared for, and boots that were fashionable five years ago which had suffered a great deal of wear.

When she looked back, she was dismayed to see the man was still there. She knew most of the local residents by sight and his was not a familiar face. He had a moustache that looked more like an old broom cut to size and tufty black eyebrows that looked like they were trying to push the hat brim off his forehead.

"Good morning," she said, straightening up as best she

could whilst supporting her increasingly limp brother. "May I help you?"

The man snorted something back up his nose that had been making a bid for freedom and cleared his throat. "Just deliverin' a letter. Live 'ere, do ya?"

She saw the envelope in his hand. "I do. Is the letter for my father?"

The man's rebellious eyebrows twitched with excitement. "Didn't know he had a daughter. 'E didn't mention that." He grinned, revealing a set of yellowed teeth that looked like they'd been crammed into his mouth in a hurry and left in disarray.

"I shall pass it on to him, but please excuse us. I need to take my brother inside now."

She waited for him to come down the three steps that separated the front door from the pavement, but the man didn't move. He just stood there, leering, as if he were trying to see through her winter coat and shawl. When a moan slipped from Ben's mouth, Charlotte lost her patience with the stranger and started up the steps, expecting him to doff his hat and make an apology. He did neither, waiting until she was squeezed in front of the door next to him, Ben on the step below. The stranger smelt of waxed cotton left in a damp box too long, and his breath was worse. Sardines for breakfast could only explain part of the stench.

He held out the letter, pincered between a grimy thumb and finger poking from fingerless gloves. "It's most important he receives this today," the man said in a mock formal tone. "Most. Important."

Charlotte took it, and much to her relief, the man descended the steps with the lopsided gait of an elegant drunkard. "Nearly there, darling," she whispered to her brother as she fumbled for the key. She knew her father had a meeting with a publisher this morning and Mother was delivering a dress she'd finished making, then taking tea with a friend who was also convalescing from a bout of illness. There was such a lot of it about at this time of year.

Soon enough, Ben was lying down on the sofa—neither of them had the strength to get him up the stairs—and the kettle was heating on the stove. Charlotte sat in the kitchen, trembling with fatigue and regretting the excursion. It had been pure vanity on her part, and she must do better. She would allow herself a cup of tea and a slice of the sponge cake Mother had baked the day before, then she would dust the living room and beat the rugs. She had no love for domestic labour, but it had to be done.

The letter rested on the table next to her. The jagged scrawl on the front read nothing more than MR J. GUNN but even that seemed to have been written with disdain.

Charlotte couldn't stop staring at it. She was convinced it couldn't possibly contain anything that would benefit her family or make her father happy. But that was just an assumption, based on the man who'd delivered it, surely? Perhaps it was a commission.

She cut herself a slice of cake, checked on Ben, who was snoring softly from beneath the crocheted blanket she'd drawn over him, and frowned at the kettle, wishing it would boil faster. Within moments steam plumed from the spout, spitting water onto the hot plate.

"Damn and blast!" Charlotte whispered, grabbing the tea towel so she could lift it from the stove. She had to be more careful! The morning's events had evidently shaken her more than she realised.

Once the small teapot was filled and covered by a tea cosy, Charlotte found herself staring at the letter again. Before she had even realised she'd made up her mind, she was holding the envelope over the wisp of steam curling up from the kettle's spout. She bit her lip as the flap curled free from the loosened gum, telling herself that it was just to ensure all was well and that nothing unsavoury was being sent to her father. He was a nervous man. It was her duty to protect him.

There was a single sheet of paper inside, of cheap stock:

6 New Road,
Whitechapel
London
20th November, 1850

Mr Gunn,

Our records show that you have not paid the last two instalments of your debt repayment. You were informed of the consequences of failure to repay when you secured the loan. You have until noon on 22th November to repay the outstanding amount in full, along with the interest incurred, otherwise steps will be taken to recover the amount.

Yours sincerely,
Mr P. Compton
Anchor Financial Services

Charlotte sat heavily in the chair, making it creak in protest. Debt? Her father hadn't mentioned anything about taking out a loan, let alone being unable to repay one. He said that he'd paid Ben's recent university fees with money from a commission. Even then, it hadn't been enough, though no one had actually broken that to him. Ben had written to her only a fortnight after starting his studies, confiding in her that he hadn't got enough money to last until the end of term and asking her to find the right moment to speak to their father about sending more money. Knowing how much the household had tightened its belt to send Ben away to train as a civil engineer, Charlotte resolved to support him financially from her own savings. She'd had to tell Ben the truth, so it didn't come out in conversation once he was home again, neither of them knowing that would only be a month later.

They had both agreed it was better that Father and Mother didn't know she'd sent him money. She'd offered to find work many times, but both of them were adamant that she would be spared what they had to endure as children. At least as an illustrator, Charlotte could earn money from a profession that didn't have any visible effect on her hands or give any other indications. She'd secretly topped up the caddy that held the household funds without her mother noticing, thanks to her disinterest in keeping good books, whilst squirrelling away the rest for her marriage. Now all of her savings had been spent supporting Ben, so there was no way she could pay the debt off for her father.

Charlotte made a mental note of the address on the letter, resealed the envelope and poured the tea. She knew how hard her father worked, and it was a testament to his talent and perseverance that he was able to provide for the family; many illustrators barely supported themselves, let alone a wife and two children. They lived in a small house which was so much better than the cramped lodgings they'd grown up in, and neither Ben nor Charlotte had been sent to find work as children, unlike so many others. Whilst they all hoped Ben would forge a good career and be able to support their parents when they got older, Charlotte had her doubts. Ben's health was poor, and it was up to her to make sure he had the time and space and care to restore himself to health again. If Father developed that tic again, the one that made his eye twitch when under pressure, Ben would think it was his fault and try to go back to university too soon. He'd already had to abandon an apprenticeship in Newcastle thanks to ill health. If he went back to university before he was fully fit, he might make himself so ill that continuing his studies would be rendered impossible.

It would be less of a strain on the household when she married and moved out, but George said that he wanted to wait until he'd been promoted, so they could afford to rent in a better area of London than where he lived now. She knew she'd receive royalties on the *Other Magicks* collection, but that wouldn't be for months and now, Father only had days. The thought of him in debtor's prison made her feel nauseous.

She couldn't talk to Mother about it all; she hated any

hints that the real world was harsher than she liked to believe, and besides, any suggestion that their earnings were inadequate was always met with shrill protestations. No. Charlotte knew she had to find a solution, and the only way that was going to happen was speaking to the lenders of the loan. She wasn't sure whether they could be reasoned with, but if she could only find out the amount, she might be able to dash off a quick commission to cover an instalment at least.

Charlotte dashed off a quick note for Ben to find when he woke up, put her coat back on and went off in search of the address, the letter tucked deep in a pocket where it could do no harm.

Chapter 3

CHARLOTTE REGRETTED her hasty decision to find the debt collector's office when she reached New Road, Whitechapel. It was not the sort of area she would normally choose to visit alone.

The houses were crammed in tight together, the street between them dark even at noon, and a mangy-looking dog was sniffing a pile of rubbish at the far end of the street. Old newspapers rendered down to little more than drifts of dark grey pulp smudged the places where the houses met the pavement. She could hear a man and a woman shouting obscenities at each other in one of the houses to the left, whilst another dog barked almost constantly in a house to the right.

Hesitating at the end of the street, Charlotte was just about to leave when she spotted a dirty brass plaque fixed to the wall of one of the houses, next to the front door. Number six—the one she recalled from the letter. Charlotte lifted the hem of her crinoline as best she could and went closer. The brass was dull and smeared with grime, the words only visible thanks to the dirt the engraving had collected.

ANCHOR FINANCIAL SERVICES

She drew back and looked at the house. She was well aware that some businesses operated in residential areas—her agent's office was next door to a townhouse in Bloomsbury—but this? It looked just as run down as all the other properties in the street. What could have possessed her father to trust anyone conducting business here in matters of money?

There were greyed lace curtains in the only window at ground level and no glass in the front door. It looked as though no one had been inside for months. Trying hard not to let herself be swayed by outward appearances—perhaps there was a perfectly reasonable explanation—Charlotte rapped on the door as loudly as she could.

There was no answer. She was momentarily relieved, but then realised that it would mean having to return and she didn't want to step foot in this street ever again. A narrow, smelly alleyway ran down the side of the house with an arched brickwork facade that joined to the house on the other side of the cut through. An old cat sat staring at her from beneath the arch. She took once last look up and down the street, just in case the man who delivered the letter was on his way back, and then went down the alleyway to see if there was a yard behind the house. Perhaps the business owner was taking a break, sitting on the back step like she did sometimes.

There was a small backyard, surrounded by a brick wall that she had no hope of scaling and a sturdy-looking back gate that was taller than her. But at the end of the alleyway there was an abandoned perambulator with only three wheels. When Charlotte stood on top of it, she could see over the wall and into the small yard covered by cracked flagstones. There was a back door and a window, through which she could see someone inside. Perhaps they simply hadn't heard her knock?

Charlotte jumped down, went to the gate and tried the latch. It didn't lift. Frustrated, she banged the flat of her hand against it and heard a pin clatter to the ground on the other side. When she tried the latch again, it opened. Grinning, she went inside, closed the gate behind her and knocked on the back door.

Still no response. Charlotte moved over to the window and cupped her hands to the glass to peer inside. There was definitely a man in there, standing next to an iron-barred cell that made her twitch with surprise. It looked like something from London Zoo, designed to hold an animal, and seemed totally incongruous with the very normal room it sat within. Then it occurred to her that it could be a place to hold debtors before they were brought before a magistrate. She shivered. Was this her father's fate?

Mustering the last of her courage, Charlotte rapped on the glass. It was so dirty, perhaps the man inside hadn't noticed her.

He just continued to stare at the cage, unmoving. She couldn't make him out very well in the dingy room, through filthy glass, but she could only assume he had some sort of hearing impediment. After trying once more to get his attention, Charlotte decided to go home.

She went out the way she came in, back through the alleyway, ignoring the way the cat hissed at her when she passed. There was a woman leaning out of the window of the house she passed earlier, watching a man running off.

"And don't you darken my door again, 'Arry Barker, else I'll give you what for!"

Charlotte waited until the man was out of sight before leaving the alleyway. As much as she hoped the woman wouldn't see her, it seemed that luck wasn't of a mind to favour her today.

"Dunno what the likes of you is doin' 'ere," said the woman, scratching a mole at the top of one of her huge, doughy breasts threatening to burst from their confines. "But I wouldn't go anywhere near that place." The woman jutted her chin at the house Charlotte had just been looking into.

"Why do you say that?" Charlotte asked, aware of how soft and quiet her own voice sounded in comparison to the woman's harsh rasp.

"Thems what go in there like this"—the woman held a hand up, fingers pointing at the sky—"come out like this"—she tipped her hand until the palm was horizontal. "Carried out in a box. Ten of 'em last month, you mark my words. You get off 'ome to wherever it is you live, and don't come back."

Charlotte didn't need any more encouragement. She bobbed a nervous curtsey of thanks, realised that was probably the most ridiculous thing to do and hurried off to the sound of the woman's creaking laughter.

Chapter 4

AS SOON AS SHE SAW George, Charlotte knew she'd made the right decision to go to her fiancé's office rather than straight home. The woman's warning about how people died at that house had clung to her like wet clothes, making her feel shivery and in need of comfort. The thought of going back home and trying to work out what to say to her father—even whether she should pass the letter on—made her feel anxious. When she saw an omnibus heading towards Piccadilly, she'd hopped on that instead. It was the one she took to meet George for lunch sometimes, and the familiarity of it made her feel better.

George was calm and dependable. He never, ever got ill. He wasn't particularly tall, nor particularly strong, but he was kind and caring and he loved her. She stood in the doorway to the office, taking a moment to examine his profile. He might not be the most handsome man in London, but he had a strong chin and a splendid set of mutton chops that put many others to shame, and he always groomed his hair well. It fell in loose waves to his collar, a shining dark brown, with a few locks that flopped down as he was bent over the huge book he wrote in. She smiled at the way his tongue poked out from between his lips as he concentrated and waited patiently for his pen to return to the inkwell before alerting him to her presence. He concentrated so deeply, she'd learnt never to speak whilst the nib was scratching across the page; otherwise, he would jump and make an ugly mark that he'd fret over for days.

Just as he reached for the inkwell, Charlotte coughed quietly. George's head snapped round and his brown eyes crinkled at the corners as he smiled broadly at her. "Charlotte! What a splendid surprise!" He rested his pen and came over to her to kiss her hand.

Charlotte's toes curled in her boots at the feel of his lips through her gloves. "Where's Mr Dougherty?"

"He has the 'flu!" George said cheerily. "I wouldn't wish it on anyone, of course, but it has been so peaceful here. I've cleared all the backlog from the merging of the parishes and this afternoon I'll have time to work on my personal project. I'm certain that I'll be able to present it when I apply for registrar. Don't you agree?"

George's personal project was another reason she'd decided to visit. She'd always felt it was rather morbid and didn't like talking about it very much, but it seemed to make him happy. "Isn't it rather outside a registrar's remit?"

"We record births, deaths and marriages, my dear. It seems such a waste to not track the information in a more useful manner than limited summary reports. And the distribution and frequency of deaths tell us so much more than people think! John and I were talking about it just the other day—oh, did you hear? He's been accepted into the Royal College of Physicians!"

Charlotte smiled, glad for George's friend who had some very strange ideas about the transmission of illness. "George, there's a word you've mentioned before, relating to your project, that I wanted to ask you about." The way his eyes brightened was simply adorable. "Um . . . clustering? Is that the right one?"

"You mean when several deaths occur in a tight, localised area or over a very short period of time?"

"Yes, that's it. I . . . I overheard a lady on the Piccadilly omnibus talking about a property in New Road, Whitechapel. She was . . . telling her friend that people who go there alive leave in a coffin."

George's eyebrows shot up. "Good grief! What a subject to discuss on public transport. Is that why you look so pale? Come and sit down, dear." He led her to his chair. She was so glad his supervisor was unwell, and immediately felt guilty for thinking so.

"Thank you. Yes, it was rather unpleasant. But then I thought of you. Oh! Heavens, that sounds terrible! What

I mean to say is that I thought of your project, and how what she talked about sounds like a cluster and . . ."

"And so you came here straightaway to tell me?" At her nod, he gave her the sweetest smile. "That's so thoughtful." He went to a shelf, plucked down a huge leather-bound tome and looked something up. "I thought so . . ." he muttered and replaced it. "That parish was in the backlog. Can you indulge me for a few moments whilst I find the record?"

Charlotte nodded and let herself lean back in the chair. She watched the wheels of the carriages clattering by from the window, appreciating for the first time how strange it was to work in a basement office with only a small window out to the street. No wonder George was always keen to meet her at lunchtime for a stroll outside; working down here by gaslight was not particularly pleasant.

The local clock tower chimed eleven o'clock and she listened to the different tones of the bells ringing out across the city, forming its own beautiful harmony. She wondered which magus was responsible for that tower and whether the baker's son would specialise in clocks and fine machinery once he was tested. Perhaps one day he would be responsible for timepieces across the city, as the most powerful magi were, able to work the magic necessary to keep perfect time across disparate devices.

She sighed, wondering where the poor boy was now and whether his mother would be able to cope without him.

No matter how hard she tried, Charlotte couldn't stop her thoughts returning to the barred cell in the back room of that awful house. Without knowing the amount her father owed, she couldn't calculate whether a commission would be enough to get him out of trouble. And what about the interest on the loan mentioned in the letter? Did that mean more needed to be paid back over time? She wasn't certain. With no one at the property, the only option was to ask her father directly, but the mere thought of it made her cringe.

All the mental churning wasn't going to change the basic fact that if she actually came clean about what she was, her family's financial troubles would be over. Charlotte wrapped her arms about herself and chewed her lip. Perhaps her selfish desire to marry and have children had to be put aside for the good of her family.

"Here we are!" George cheered from the doorway, carrying a huge book. "What was the address again?"

"Number six, New Road, Whitechapel."

"She was very exact, then?"

Charlotte nodded.

"That makes it more likely to be true," he said, not suspecting her flimsy story about a woman on the omnibus at all. Dear, sweet, trusting George.

He flipped through a few pages, then retrieved a notebook from his desk, pausing to place a tender kiss on her cheek before returning to his work. Charlotte rested her head on the back of the chair and the next moment, George was shaking her by the shoulder.

"Charlotte? Wake up, dear. I have something interesting to show you."

She blinked, briefly disoriented. She was more tired than she'd realised. Nursing her brother always took it out of her. She went to George's side and saw that he'd slipped book marks into at least a dozen places.

"It is a cluster!" he said with an excited grin. "One that I didn't notice. Over the past six months, no less than fourteen people have died at number six, New Road."

Charlotte clamped a hand over her mouth to trap the frightened squeak inside.

"All heart attacks," George went on. "All certified at the scene by Dr Stephen Ledbetter, who is one of the more reliable practitioners. He covers Whitechapel and a couple of other parishes."

He opened the book to show one of the death certificates, pointing out the doctor's signature.

"Fourteen in six months? Isn't that"—Charlotte tried to swallow away the lump in her throat—"rather unusual?"

"It depends. It might be a private clinic for those with

heart trouble, though unlikely in that area."

"It's a financial services company."

George frowned at her. "You didn't mention that."

"It slipped my mind. That's why the errr . . . the woman on the omnibus knew about it. Her husband . . ." Charlotte trailed off, unable to keep the lie coherent in her mind, let alone spoken aloud.

"Oh, well, that explains it," George said, oblivious. "Probably one of those shady operations where they put the thumbscrews on if someone can't repay a loan."

"Thumbscrews?" Charlotte yelped. "Like what they did to Guy Fawkes?" The thought of her father in that cell was bad enough; the speculation about him being harmed made her knees tremble.

"Not literally! But it might be that the debtor is held there before going to the magistrate. I imagine some can't take the strain and they keel over. Dreadful business, and an interesting cluster, but not the sort that Dr Snow and I are particularly interested in. No questions about miasma to address there, I fear. But I do appreciate you taking the time to come tell me about it. Good heavens, Charlotte, you really do look the worse for wear. May I suggest I hail a cab for you, to see you home? As much as I enjoy your company, I can't exploit Mr Dougherty's absence indefinitely and I do think you need a lie-down."

He was giving her the look she often gave Ben, and

she really didn't like it. No wonder Ben got so irritable when she fussed over him. But she couldn't deny that she needed to get home, even though rest would be elusive. "Thank you, George, dear. Will I see you tonight?"

He shook his head. "I have a meeting with John and a couple of his friends he's managed to bring round to his way of thinking. I do have Friday afternoon off, however. How about I collect you at lunchtime?"

Would she still be a free woman then? She forced the worry from her face and gave him her best smile. "I shall look forward to it."

Chapter 5

THE RIDE HOME in her second hansom cab of the day was not long enough for Charlotte to resolve her dilemma. Whichever decision she made, it would end in heartbreak, for both herself and someone she loved. If she stayed the silent coward, her father might end up in that cell, perhaps even dead. If she gave herself up to the Royal Society of Esoteric Arts for testing, she would save her family but lose her chance of a happy life and break George's heart in the process. But if her father died, how could she enjoy married life, knowing she could have prevented his death? When she looked at it that way, surely she had to give herself up?

The magi had wealth, yes, but hardly any freedom. A person confirmed as a magus wasn't permitted to marry, nor to pursue any interests outside those endorsed by the Royal Society, including art. She would rather be penniless than lead that sort of life. But it wasn't just the fact that she and George wouldn't be able to marry if she were recruited into the Royal Society—of which there was no doubt if she gave herself up—it was also the fact that she'd lose her autonomy. All magi were expected to do their upmost for the Empire and their own personal wishes were secondary. Not only would it be the end of her engagement, it would be the end of her career; the Society would never permit a magus to earn money from anything but the practical application of their magical arts.

Then there was the problem of fame. Fellows of the Society were regularly written about in the press, talked about over meals by people who didn't know them and sometimes approached by complete strangers on the street. Books were written about them; one of her father's latest commissions was illustrating the biography of Magus Anneline Royston. Her personal timepiece was currently in his study, one of the many objects lent by the Royal Society for an exorbitant fee. Charlotte's nose wrinkled at the thought of people drawing her personal possessions, writing about her, presuming to know her! No, she didn't have the sort of character that would serve her well in such a prominent position. But would she rather watch her father be carried off to a debtor's prison than be a magus?

No. She wouldn't.

She paid the driver and let herself into the house. As soon as she stepped inside she could hear her mother shouting in the living room. Shocked, she didn't notice

Ben sitting on the lowest stair until he reminded her to shut the front door.

"Who is Mother shouting at?" she whispered to him.

"Father," he replied.

"How could you have done this without telling me?" she heard her mother through the living room door.

Father must have told her about the debt.

"It's because of the letter that came today," Ben said. "Father didn't tell Mother what he'd done and you know what she's like about not knowing what's going on. Where have you been?"

"I went to see George," she said, putting her hand into her pocket to check that the letter about the debt was still there. She could feel the corner of the envelope prickle her palm through her gloves.

"He should have told her," Ben said. "And whilst I don't usually agree with Mother when she gets shrill, asking the Royal Society to come and make an evaluation without telling anyone is a rather—"

Charlotte felt the blood drain from her face. Tiny pinpricks of light peppered her peripheral vision as an awful high-pitched whistling sound pressed in her ears. "But . . . how did he know? Why didn't he warn me?"

She felt her back hit the inside of the front door and she used it to brace herself as she drew in a few deep breaths. Ben stood and came to her side. At least he looked better for his rest. "I'm fully prepared to undergo the test, Charlie. And it was because of the watch. He didn't warn you because . . ." He stopped. "Wait a moment. You thought he had sent for *you* to be tested. Oh, Charlie . . ."

He didn't look angry, that was something. He mostly looked concerned. Their mother's voice was getting more shrill and less comprehensible, and was doing nothing to help Charlotte restore her own balance. "Let's talk upstairs."

It felt like it took years to climb the stairs, and it still wasn't enough time to plan what she was going to say. Then she was in her room, sitting on the bed next to him. "I should have told you," she said. "But I couldn't. I don't want to be one of them, Ben, I can't imagine anything worse!"

She covered her mouth. What a thoughtless thing to say when he was soon to be tested.

"I don't feel the same way."

"But you're not a magus, Ben! We'd have known by now, surely?"

"I had no idea you believed yourself to be gifted until just now."

Gifted? Cursed, rather. "So have you been hiding it, too?"

He shrugged. "Not exactly. I just . . . didn't have any faith in my own suspicions."

Charlotte frowned. "But you have to be certain before you take the test. If you fail it, Father will be tried for false reporting. The fine alone would cripple us, and if he were jailed—"

"Credit me with some sense, Charlie. I would have refuted it and begged for the application to be withdrawn in person if I thought it were false. I don't think I'm very gifted, but the Royal Society takes in individuals with the weakest ability. Apparently some of the most powerful magi were late developers."

The lump in her throat was back and Charlotte kept swallowing in an attempt to dislodge it. Had she done something near Ben without realising and accidentally fooled him into believing he was one of them? But when he was ill, the most she did was sit at his bedside and read to him, feed him broth when he was at his weakest and fetch water. She hadn't even cooled the flannel for his brow using her . . . burden.

"But don't you want to be a civil engineer?"

Ben's smile was so sad. "Dear heart, do you really think I would complete the degree?"

"Have you been hit over the head? What makes you think that being dragged away to the Royal Society will be any easier than a degree?" Her vision blurred as tears welled up, hot and furious at their father. How dare he risk Ben's health? He knew as well as they all did that twice Ben had left the house in fine health, to live in another city and acquire a trade, and both times he'd returned gaunt and barely able to walk. "What if you fall ill again and need to come home and they don't let you? Who will look after you there?"

He reached for her hand, took it and wrapped it tightly with both his own. "I'm not going to deny that that concerns me, too. But we know things can't continue as they are. I'm a constant drain on the family—and on you! Don't you have any idea how ashamed I am to have to beg my sister for money?"

The first tear fell and splattered on her lap. "I don't mind, I'm glad to help you! I would rather send you every penny I earn than see you be dragged off by those monstrous people!"

"Darling, that's the second time you've said that. It's a formal test. No one will drag me off. I'll go willingly, and our family will be well compensated. And in a few years, when I've found my feet and chosen a specialisation, I should be able to earn far more than I ever would as a civil engineer. Mother and Father will want for nothing, and I'll be able to pay you back and help you instead!"

The tears ran faster now, stealing the words from her throat, all the strain from the morning finally being released. Her father was risking Ben's life to pay off his debts. She was of a mind to go downstairs now and—

"Charlie, if you're also gifted, don't you think you should come forward?"

She shook her head.

"It's the only decent thing to do."

"No!" She looked at him, frightened now. "Don't tell them. Please, Ben, don't tell anyone!"

He sighed. "But there's a good reason the law is the way it is. You could become a danger to everyone. George, Mother, Father."

Charlotte scowled. "That's not true. That's just been made up to frighten people into coming forward." She could feel her cheeks burning, making the tears feel cool as they slid down her face. She was always careful, she was always in control. How could she possibly be a risk to anyone?

"What sort of talk is that?" He sighed. "That's what that madman said at Speaker's Corner the other day."

"He wasn't mad!" Charlotte didn't feel it was the right time to mention that she'd gone back to listen to that man several times since she and Ben had happened across him. "He made a great deal of sense. And the things he said about what the magi do to people who don't want to be one of them . . ." She shivered.

"Whether someone with the gift wants to become a magus or not is irrelevant, Charlie. It's their duty to come forward and learn how to control what they are for the good of the Empire."

That's what he felt she should do. "I'm not one of them," she whispered. "I can't be like them."

Ben pressed his lips together. "If you came forward, too, we could be together. We could help each other through our training."

It felt like he'd grabbed a string in her heart and pulled it. She could take care of him and the family would be financially secure. It made so much sense! But then she thought of George and the end of her private life and the rest of her heartstrings pulled in the opposite direction. She shook her head, hating herself as she did it. If only she weren't so selfish!

There was an awful silence, punctuated by an occasional sniff on her part. Ben fetched her a clean handkerchief from her bedside drawer and she dabbed at her nose.

"I know you'll do the right thing, Charlie Bean," Ben said softly. "In your own time. I trust you and I won't say a word to anyone. I know what you're like. You can't be pushed into anything. You have to be ready, and it's clear that you're not."

She managed a small smile, relieved. Should she tell him about the debt? What use would it do? She had to think carefully now and find a way to get Ben through the test. "So you think you can pass their test? Do you know what they ask people to do?"

He shook his head. "No idea. Do you?"

"No. Show me what you can do. That's as good a place to start as any."

"Well..." He looked away. "I made a pen roll off a table once."

"Are you sure you didn't knock it with your elbow?"

"I was feverish at the time, so I was in bed, not at my desk. I was staring at it, thinking it had moved, and then off it went."

Charlotte blew her nose, hoping to hide her despair. "I see."

Detecting that she was far from impressed, he added, "I can make a candle flame burn brighter. That's undeniable."

She didn't agree. If he'd been staring at a flame, hoping to be a magus, he could easily have fooled himself into thinking there was a change. "Anything more than a candle flame?" When he shook his head, she said, "Well, what made Father think you were one of them?"

"Ah! Yes! The watch. The one belonging to the magus that he's been illustrating for that book about her. Remember, he showed it to us last week over dinner? Well, I confess I went and took a closer look at it whilst you were having lunch with George yesterday. I just couldn't resist! It's such an exquisite object and when would I ever get the chance to actually hold a real timepiece? Well, it turns out that when Father went back to finish his illustration, the hands were in a different position. He didn't change them; he's not permitted to open the case and I certainly didn't alter the hands so when he pressed me about it, and I confessed to examining it, the conclusion was obvious! I must have set it ticking again with latent magic."

Charlotte feared she was going to be sick. Most of the time she was happy to be constantly overlooked; it gave her such freedom to draw and paint and form her own opinions about things. Only now was she appreciating just how little her father—and Ben, to a lesser extent—noticed her and her talents. Wordlessly, she went to the wooden chest beneath the window and retrieved her sketchbook, hidden as it always was beneath her steadily growing bridal trousseau.

She took the book back to sit next to Ben and flipped to the relevant page. She turned the book to show him her detailed illustration of the timepiece's internal workings.

Ben gasped. "You drew this?" When she nodded, she saw sweat sparkle on his forehead. "I didn't change it. *You* did. It was you all along!" His hands went to his head, squeezing it. "What am I to do? You have to step forward, Charlie!

They'll understand Father's error and a prosecution can be avoided if they leave the house with a new recruit!"

Charlotte slammed the sketchbook shut. Now that Ben was falling apart, she discovered an untapped well of fortitude. One of them had to come up with a solution. "Calm down. You'll make yourself ill, and we need to think." Stunned into silence, Ben just stared at her, so she shut her eyes, focusing instead on the pounding of her heart. "I agree that it was my fault the hands moved on the watch. I should have been more careful and checked them before I put it back in the box. But that doesn't mean you can't move objects or alter a flame. If you can do those, you can pass the test."

"But if I'm only a weak candidate, they won't pay the family much compensation at all. It won't be worth it."

"One thing at a time," Charlotte replied, a plan forming. "First, light that candle whilst I put this back."

Once the sketchbook was hidden away again, she returned to Ben's side who had lit the candle she kept in a holder on her nightstand. She moved it to the other side of the room and returned to the bed. "Now try to make the flame brighter."

He stared at it and she did, too, desperate to see any change at all. When it brightened she beamed at him, but he was frowning. "That must have been you!" he said with frustration.

She couldn't deny it was a possibility. It seemed that nowadays she didn't have to really try very much at all to achieve a small effect. "I'll leave the room. You practise for a couple of minutes, and then I'll return and you can show me."

Her parents were still arguing downstairs, so Charlotte sat on the top step and rested her head on her knees. She could see a solution, but it all hinged on whether Ben had any latent ability at all. If not, she would have no choice but to put herself forward in his place. What a royal mess. Her father had taken it upon himself to find a different solution to his money woes, but she couldn't blame him for the mistake he'd made. If she'd been more honest, none of this would have happened.

There was a faint cheer from her bedroom and her heart soared. *Please, please, please be right,* she whispered to herself and went back in when he called for her.

"I did it, Charlie! Watch. I'm going to count to a secret number in my mind and then alter the flame. You tell me when you see the change."

She nodded, sitting herself beside him and actively willing herself not to try to wish any difference in the flame. Then she was scared she might accidentally suppress whatever impact he could make, so instead she concentrated on counting silently, trying to be patient. When she got to eleven, the flame brightened and stretched upwards. Ben looked at her with a huge smile. "Did you see that?"

"I did!" She cheered and threw her arms about him. They laughed in the embrace, and she felt the worst of the terror leaving her stomach. She pulled away from him, steadying herself for the ordeal ahead. "I have a plan, Ben. This is what we're going to do . . ."

Chapter 6

"WE CAN'T ASK THEM to have the plates on their laps," Mother said, twisting her handkerchief so tightly it creaked.

"We can't magically make our house or dining table any bigger, either," Charlotte said.

"But what will they think of us?"

"That we're a normal family in a small house? I don't think they're really going to care about plates and laps, are they?" Charlotte immediately regretted her tone. "I'm sorry, Mother, I didn't mean to be so rude." She understood that her mother's nerves were at breaking point, and this time, there was a genuinely good reason for it. And it was obvious that fretting over how the eminent visitors were going to be able to take tea was easier to focus on than the prospect of Ben being taken away. As soon as the thought hit Charlotte, she, too, felt tearful again. Then her mother saw and the sniffling started again. Trying her best to put her own emotions aside, Charlotte put an arm around her mother.

"I shall never forgive your father for doing this," her

mother said, dabbing at her eyes. "He should have discussed it with all of us first. I simply don't know what possessed him."

Charlotte suspected it was something to do with the debt. Perhaps the man who delivered the letter had lurked nearby afterwards and threatened Father when he returned home. After seeing the business premises, she wouldn't put it past him. "Whatever the reason, we have to make the best of it all now," Charlotte said, surprised by how steady her voice was. Perhaps if her mother was calmer, she would feel safe enough to really show how upset she was, but right now, she had to be the strong one. "I suggest we lay out the tea on the table folded up in the living room, against the wall, and put the dining chairs out amongst the living room chairs. Then there will be somewhere for everyone to sit and it will be clear that it's a buffet, so no one will mind." Charlotte didn't have anything left within her heart to care about whether anyone would be upset by their inability to cater for more than two guests at a time; it was so much less important than the reason they were coming. But she was determined to settle her mother as much as possible, and eliminating these seemingly irrelevant obstacles was the best way to achieve that.

"You are such a sensible girl," her mother said, kissing her on the cheek. "Whatever will I do when you marry George? Oh . . . both of my children will soon be gone . . ."

"I'm not going anywhere yet," Charlotte said, reaching even the limit of her patience. "Besides, we will be living very nearby, all being well. And once Ben is a fully recognised magus, he'll visit, too. Let's get the tea laid out."

There was no denying that the practical task was good for both of them. They moved furniture, carried things between rooms and sternly told Ben to lie down and rest when he came to help. Charlotte stayed on her feet when her mother had a brief sit-down, fearing that if she stopped, she'd never get up again. Just as she was starting to worry that her father had fallen afoul of the debt collectors, she heard the front door open.

"I'm back!" Father called from the hallway. "The bakery was closed! I had to walk to the one with that awful dog that growls when you point at the loaf you want."

Charlotte grimaced. She should have warned him their usual one would be closed. She wondered how the baker was coping. Then she was swept up in panicked sandwich making, lamp lighting and managing her mother's worries about whether to cut off the crusts and before she knew it, there was a knock on the door.

It was like someone cast a spell over the house, freezing them all where they stood. In the silence, Mother looked over to her with reddened eyes, the little colour left in her cheeks draining away. Charlotte drew in a deep breath, imagining that this must be what it was like for a singer before going out onto a stage. A glance in the mirror reassured her that her dark brown hair was neat, the bun at the back still tight and the plaits on either side of her parting even. She looked at herself with the same brown eyes as her brother's, the shape so familiar because of talking to him, rather than staring at herself. She looked pale and tired but at least her eyes weren't bloodshot. Small mercies. She untied her apron, smoothed down the front of her dress and checked that the waist pleats of her crinoline were neat. Then when she was fully ready, she reminded her mother to take off her apron and went out into the hallway.

Father was staring at the door as Ben came down the stairs, smoothing his hair back into place where the pillow had pushed it into disarray. Charlotte looked at her father, noting how his hands shook. He was a tall, thin man, someone a caricaturist would sketch as an undertaker, rather than an artist. His hair was fully grey at the temples now but still brown elsewhere, and unlike many men his age, he still had a full head of it. She saw how he'd tried to tame it with some hair oil, with limited success. "Father?"

"What if I've made a terrible mistake, Charlie?"

Charlotte tried to swallow but her mouth and throat

were too dry. "It may not amount to very much, but I don't think you have, Papa."

She hadn't called him that for so long and it jarred his gaze from the door to meet her eyes. She smiled at him, wanting to show him he wasn't alone, and then there was another knock which made them all jump, breaking the moment.

Father opened it to reveal a man standing on the doorstep, wearing a bold red coat that looked like it would cost more than their coal bill for a cold winter. His skin was dark brown, as were his eyes, and he wore a hat similar in style to those worn by the Beefeaters at the Tower of London, only with an additional red triangle stitched within the circle embroidery at the front of the hat. "Mr Jeremiah Gunn?"

Charlotte watched her father nod and appreciated just how awestruck he was.

"I act with the authority of Her Majesty, Queen Victoria, and on behalf of Her Majesty, I greet you and thank you for your vigilance. Your co-operation has been noted. I am to be addressed as Master Judicant for the duration of this process."

Father just nodded again.

"May I come in?"

When her father nodded dumbly a third time, Charlotte stepped forwards. "Good afternoon, Master Judicant. My name is Charlotte, this is my brother, Benjamin, and my mother, Edith. Please do come in. May I take your coat and hat?"

Master Judicant smiled at her and seemed human again after the terrifying formality of his introduction. Charlotte liked the way his smile made the corners of his eyes crinkle. "Thank you, Miss Gunn." He shrugged off the coat, revealing a black frock coat with the same symbol from his hat embroidered on the lapels. The plump cravat at his throat was pinned with something red that sparkled, his collar starched to perfection. Beneath the hat his curly hair was cut very short with a few grey strands sprinkled throughout.

No one so finely dressed had ever been in their house before. Charlotte found herself noticing the threadbare patch on the runner and the cracked floor tile near the front door that Father had been meaning to replace for as long as she could remember. She took the coat—so heavy!—and the hat and arranged them on the coat stand, in such a way as to hide the crack in the plaster behind it, as Master Judicant shook hands with her father and Ben.

"So you're the Latent?" she heard him say to her brother. "Older than usual. Most manifest in their early teens."

Ben looked momentarily panicked, before Father said, "He's been away, studying."

"Even so . . ."

"Ben has been unwell, too," Charlotte said, going to Ben's side. "Long illnesses with extended convalescences. He didn't really have an opportunity to show anything."

She ignored the glare from her father; it was all going to come out one way or another, and when the authority of the Crown was involved, it was best to be as truthful as possible. When it came to her brother's medical history, at least.

It seemed to satisfy Master Judicant, who nodded and then cast his eye over the small hallway and up the stairs. It was as if they were all holding their breath, waiting for some sort of judgement. Mother, who seemed to shake herself back into life again after being statue-like since the door had opened, smiled at him. "Where do you come from, Master Judicant?"

The man raised an eyebrow at her. "I was at the Tower this morning, the Palace this afternoon and then I made my way here." At her slight frown he added. "I live in Kensington."

"Forgive me, I meant the place of your birth."

Charlotte could see Master Judicant's jaw clench, and if they'd been seated around a table, she would have kicked her mother's shin. "I was born in Colchester, Madam, though I hardly see why that should be relevant to the testing of your son."

"Will you be testing me, sir?" Ben asked, eager to shift the focus away from Mother.

Master Judicant shook his head. "No, that is the province of the magi who will be with us very shortly. It's my role to see that the testing is carried out in accordance with the law and without any interference from external parties. Should the claim prove to be false, I am tasked with executing the course of justice."

Charlotte saw her father's Adam's apple bob up and down several times. "How long will the test take?"

"Today is a preliminary consultation to determine whether there are grounds for a formal test. Your son will be interviewed by each of the magi who represent the three colleges of magic. Should he satisfy them that he does indeed have latent ability, they will return tomorrow for the tests proper. Should he pass, the three magi will withdraw to consider the offer they wish to make to your son, incorporating the compensation made to your family. He must accept one of the offers, as decreed by law. Once he has chosen the college to which he will submit himself for training, he will leave with the appropriate magus, and the payment will be made to your family within seven days. Ensuring that payment is made in a timely fashion is the last of my duties."

"He's tested here?" Father asked in surprise.

"Yes, Mr Gunn. The magi will explain why, I'm sure."

Master Judicant paused at the sound of a voice on the other side of the door, followed by a smart rap upon it, made by a cane. "Ah, here they are."

Charlotte was nearest to the door and took it upon herself to open it. Her father seemed to be in mild shock, Ben was gripping the bannister and she felt any support he could gain from it should be maintained, and she didn't trust Mother to greet them without causing offence. As she opened the door, she realised there was more than one person outside and that they were in the middle of a conversation. A man with a deep voice and a broad northern accent was in the middle of relating something.

". . . and I told him, if he can't tell the difference between them, he should get back on that train and go back to where he bloody well came from. Prat." The man was huge, barrel-chested and sported an impressive salt-and-pepper beard. He wore a stovepipe hat that was so tall she couldn't see the top of it past the doorframe and a half-caped coat made of a boldly patterned green-and-brown tweed. His scowl didn't lift at the sight of her. "Who are you, then? The maid?"

Charlotte blushed. "My name is Charlotte Gunn. I live here."

"Gunn? I thought the Latent was a bloke."

"Get out of the way, Ledbetter," came a female voice

69

from behind him. A woman pushed her way past the huge man, almost knocking him off the step in the process. "Forgive my colleague's poor manners," she said, extending a gloved hand which Charlotte shook awkwardly. "He's forgotten how to talk to people who aren't magi or staff." She had a softer northern accent, and a cold smile. Her auburn hair was swept back from her face and pinned rather eccentrically, reminding Charlotte of a portrait of Queen Elizabeth I she'd seen at a gallery. She wore a beautiful coat made of deep blue velvet with a high collar. "My name is Magus Lillian Ainsworth of the college of Thermaturgy. That rude oaf was Magus William Ledbetter, of the college of Dynamics. In you go, Ledbetter, make some room for us all, why don't you?"

Ledbetter? That was the same surname as the doctor who'd signed off the deaths at that awful house. Could they be related? Charlotte caught her thoughts and silently chided herself. It was a very common name. How could she be so fanciful as to think the two could be connected?

Ledbetter squeezed past her, muttering to himself, and forced Charlotte to press herself against the wall to allow him into the house. Only when he was inside did Charlotte even notice the third person on the steps.

"And this," Magus Ainsworth said, waving a blue velvet hand over her shoulder, "is Magus Thomas Hopkins of the college of Fine Kinetics." Satisfied that introductions had been made, Magus Ainsworth headed inside without further invitation, pausing only to whisper, "He'll try to kiss your hand, just to warn you," in Charlotte's ear as she passed.

The gentleman left outside was quite simply the most handsome man Charlotte had even seen. In fact, *handsome* seemed such an impoverished descriptor that she immediately discarded the word from her mind and settled upon *beautiful* instead. From the perfect cupid's bow of his lips (that she ached to draw) to the chiselled jawline, she wouldn't have been surprised if someone told her he was actually an artist's sculpture made flesh as a result of some Faustian pact. He was wearing a burgundy coat with a black satin lapel and black leather gloves. He moved to the top step, smiling at her warmly, a few stray blond curls escaping from beneath the brim of his top hat. His eyes were so blue it was like they had a light of their own, the irises edged in a darker shade, as if God himself had made efforts to contain their colour. He was younger than the other two magi by several years, closer to her in age, yet he had the bearing of a man with supreme self-assuredness. He sported no moustache and had only the most discreet sideburns, but somehow it seemed right for him to be clean-shaven and his beauty to be admired unimpeded.

"Miss Gunn, a pleasure," he said. His voice was soft and deep and it seemed like she felt it rather than heard it. There was no hint of a regional accent; in fact, he was better spoken than most of the people she talked to every day. He scooped up her right hand, the leather of his glove warm, and pressed his lips to her skin. Her toes curled so quickly the leather of her shoes squeaked and she prayed he hadn't heard it. His lips felt like silk worn against the body, softened and warmed by contact, and she felt the most alarming blush stretch up her throat and into her cheeks. "You must be the Latent's sister?"

She nodded, having lost the ability to speak. Surely he could see her pulse hammering the skin of her neck so violently?

"There's no need to be afraid," he said, still holding her hand long after his lips had left it. "This could be the beginning of a marvellous new life for him, and for your family."

He was beautiful, but not beautiful enough to persuade her of that. He released her hand after staring into her eyes a little too long, and she felt like a blancmange just turned out of its mould. She managed to make way for him to enter and stole a moment to gather herself as she closed the front door.

Master Judicant made sure that all the introductions were seen to as Charlotte concentrated on not staring at

Magus Hopkins. She took their coats and worried that the stand would collapse under the weight of all the expensive fabric. She was glad when they all went into the living room and she had something other than Magus Hopkins to focus on. She volunteered to see to the tea, just so she could keep herself busy as everyone helped themselves to sandwiches. Making sure she didn't make the hot water boil again was enough to ground her in something more laudable than simpering over the magus. When she passed a cup of tea to him, the cup rattled in the saucer and made her blush again, but he simply smiled sweetly at her. That didn't help at all. Ben gave her a pointed look when she came over to sit next to him, and if he'd noticed the effect Magus Hopkins was having on her, there was every chance Mother had, too. A quick glance in her direction reassured her that Mother was suffering from a similar affliction.

"So," Magus Ledbetter said after devouring three sandwiches in as many bites. "Did Master Judicant tell you what's what?"

"Yes, sir," Father replied.

"And it were you that reported this lad?"

"Yes, sir."

"So it's your neck on the block if he's not what you thought, then?"

"Take no notice of 'im," said Magus Ainsworth, throwing a glare in Ledbetter's direction. "Tell us why you made the report, Mr Gunn. Your son's older than the average Latent."

Her father told them the same as they'd told Master Judicant.

"Do you have any questions? Or any concerns that we can allay?" Magus Hopkins asked when the story was finished. His voice was so soothing.

"Will it be dangerous?" Mother asked, and he shook his head.

"No, madam, I can assure you that your son will be perfectly safe throughout. We will each set him a test which employs a technique used within our specialisms. He'll be shown how to do it first, and we will be nearby when he attempts it himself."

"You won't be in the room with me?"

"We need to be certain that it's you, not us," said Magus Ainsworth. "Master Judicant will be present for all of it, and he'll make the observations during your tests. We'll wait outside and be on hand if anything goes wrong—which it won't, but that's part of the rules."

"Has anything ever gone wrong?" Mother asked.

"Only the once, since I started testin'," said Magus Ledbetter. "It were the family's fault, though. Waited as long as they could before reporting the child, then we had to test 'er when she was practically wild. Almost burnt the house down. Bloody palaver, that was."

Charlotte tried to work out if he was telling them as some sort of comment about Ben's age. "I'm far from wild, sir," Ben said, obviously thinking the same as her.

"Glad to hear it," Ledbetter said. "We don't want you to hold back, mind you. The better you test, the more we pay, simple as that."

"Will we have a chance to say good-bye, before Ben leaves?" Father asked.

"Of course!" Ainsworth said. "We're not jailers, Mr Gunn. He's not being taken off to the gallows, is he, now? But we do insist that the apprentice leaves within the hour, once the offer has been accepted. It's important to start right away, and it's best for the family, too. We test at home to give the Latent the best chance of performing well. We've found that being in a familiar environment acts as a sort of focus and helps with nerves, too. But the sooner the apprentice learns the correct way to manage their talent, the better. Especially in your case, young man. Late bloomer that you are."

"Nowt wrong with that," Ledbetter said, grasping for another round of sandwiches from the table beside him. Charlotte had wondered why he'd headed straight for that particular chair. "I didn't manifest anythin' till I were nineteen years of age, and then it were only a trifle. I were workin' too hard in't pit to even notice. Four and twenty years later, I'm one of the wealthiest men in Lancashire and one of the best Dynamic practitioners you'll ever get to meet. The mills I run with my esoteric arts are the most efficient in the Empire."

"There's an inverse correlation between his power and his modesty," Hopkins said. "Scholars have written papers on it."

"Less of that, you," Ledbetter said through a mouthful of cucumber and crumbs. "If I 'ad a voice like yours, I'd keep me trap shut, lest anyone think the worst of me."

"Oh, give over, the both of you," Ainsworth said. "Ledbetter, you know as well as I do that whilst Hopkins might sound like a toff, there isn't a noble bone in his body."

"There's no nobility in your blood, is there?" Ledbetter asked Ben, fixing his eyes on him.

"Not as far as I know," Ben said, looking to his parents.

"My grandfather was a farmer," said his father. "I don't know much about the family before him, because it wasn't very interesting. And my wife's family were in service. Not a drop of noble blood on either side."

"You're doing well for a farmer's grandson," Ledbetter commented, looking around the room.

"My mother inherited money from the family she was in service to all her life, which she passed on to us in her will," Charlotte's mother said. "It improved our circumstances a great deal. And my husband is a very successful illustrator. We are quite comfortable."

Charlotte studied her hands, noting how her mother hadn't mentioned the sewing she did every night by candlelight to bring in more money. She made out that they didn't need any money at all.

All three of the magi nodded, satisfied that their lower-middle-class lifestyle was due to good luck, rather than nobility fallen on hard times. Charlotte knew that none of the nobility had ever passed a test, and only a very small number of them had even been put forward in the early days of the Royal Society. It seemed that fate dictated that only one sort of privilege be bestowed upon an individual at birth: magic or nobility. She wondered what would happen if someone proved to have both.

"Do you not have any concerns, Miss Gunn?"

Charlotte jolted when Hopkins addressed her. "No," she replied.

"None at all?" he pressed, and Ben looked at her expectantly.

"None, thank you," she said, blushing again.

"Well, I don't know about the rest of you, but I'm keen to get started," Ledbetter said, and then belched loudly. "Thems were very nice sandwiches, by the way. Is there any cake?"

Now it was Mother's turn to blush. "I'm so sorry, I

didn't have time to bake one. There's some sponge cake, but not enough for everyone."

"That'll do nicely, love," he said with a grin. "Bring it to me in t'other room—I take it you've got a dining room?"

"I'll move some chairs back in there," Father said, not mentioning that it was also where he and Mother did their work.

"Only three chairs needed," Ledbetter said. "I'll go first. I've got to be back at the Guildhall by six." He made it to the door before turning to his fellow magi. "Oh, did you two have any more pressing appointments?" When both shook their heads, Ledbetter followed Father and Ben out of the room. Master Judicant finished his tea and thanked Charlotte when she took his cup and saucer. Her smile was rewarded by the crinkling around his eyes again, and she felt somewhat better that he was going to be present throughout. She would have hated the thought of Ben alone in a room with one of the magi. Then he left, and she realised she was alone with two of them.

"I . . . I'll just go and help my mother," she said to Magus Ainsworth and hurried from the room.

Chapter 7

CHARLOTTE BUSIED HERSELF IN the kitchen, finding any excuse she could to avoid having to go back to the living room. Her mother took the last slice of cake to Magus Ledbetter and then came back to the kitchen looking so tired that Charlotte sent her up to bed to lie down. "It's not like the magi want to talk to us, Mother," she replied to her protestations. "They'll be much happier waiting in the living room by themselves, without having to make small talk with the likes of us."

Soon afterwards, Father came to the door. "Is there any tea left in the pot?"

"It's rather stewed but good enough." Charlotte poured them both a small cup and he took his gratefully. "Have you come to hide in here, too?" she asked and he smiled.

"Would you think the worse of me if I did?"

"Not at all."

He sat next to her, both with their backs to the stove, the little wooden stool making his long legs fold up at such an angle that he had to balance his tea cup on his knee. "What do you think of them?"

Charlotte shrugged, not wanting to give all of her honest opinion. "They have very nice coats."

There was a pause. "I'm sorry I didn't tell you first," he said, quietly enough for her to hear the crackle of the coal in the stove behind her. "I should have. Clearly. But it all happened so quickly. I thought I'd have time to discuss with everyone, give you fair warning, but they said the consultation always happens right away."

"It didn't occur to you to tell us what you planned to do *before* you reported Ben?"

He stared down into his tea. "I should have. I wasn't really thinking very carefully at the time."

Charlotte felt the pressure of things left unsaid building in her chest. She took a deep breath, keeping them inside as best she could. If he wanted to talk to her about the debt, it was up to him to raise the subject. If she did so, he would be humiliated.

She sipped her tea and wondered how Ben was coping. She imagined George bent over a book in his office, his quill scratching across the page. She thought of the cage and the strange man standing there, just staring at it. *No less than fourteen people have died ... Probably one of those shady operations where they put the thumbscrews on ...*

"Papa, I know about the debt!" She didn't look at him, even though she could see his mouth drop open from the corner of her eye. "A horrible man was here this morning, delivering a letter and . . . oh, please forgive me, Papa, but I read it! He was such an awful man, I . . ."

"Oh, Charlie. What must you think of me?"

After setting her cup down on the table, Charlotte twisted round until she faced him. "How much did you borrow?"

"I shouldn't discuss such things with you! You're my daughter!"

"Papa, I know now. I won't tell anyone, not even Mother if that's what you wish, but please tell me the truth. I need to know all of it, otherwise I'll just imagine far worse."

Her father looked down, unable to meet her eyes. "Twenty pounds. That's what I borrowed. I couldn't afford all of Ben's fees. I thought I could pay it back with a commission that was being negotiated at the time, but the publisher chose another illustrator at the last minute and it all fell through. I couldn't pay it back in time, so I negotiated paying it back in instalments. Then another commission fell through and I missed the last two payments. I . . . I just seem to be cursed." He drew in a deep breath. "Now I owe forty pounds."

Charlotte's stomach churned and she swallowed several times, hoping everything would stay where it should. "Forty pounds? Oh, Papa." It would take so many commissions to earn that much money.

He rested his head in his hands and for a dreadful moment Charlotte thought he was about to weep. He sucked in a breath and looked at her once more. "Ben will complete his test and our fortunes will change. I don't want you to think the money was the only reason I reported him! I had to do it, as I'm sure you understand. It's just that the debt collectors threatened me and I panicked and when I saw the timepiece had changed . . . I just didn't think, Charlie. I just went and did it."

"But the letter said you need to pay by noon on Friday. Master Judicant said the family would be compensated within seven days but we don't even know how much it will be!"

"I'll explain that to them."

"But Papa, people die at that place! You mustn't go there."

"What people? Where?"

Reluctantly, she told him what she'd discovered from George. For the sake of his nerves, she left out the part about actually going to the place in person.

His face was ashen. "I shall write them a letter," he said, standing up. "Yes, that's what I'll do. I'll write it now and post it right away. Surely they should understand that they'll get the money and they won't want to do anything to jeopardise that."

Charlotte stood, too, and embraced him. "It will all be straightened out. And you're a wonderful illustrator and things will improve, I'm sure of it. That publisher was a fool to turn you down."

He kissed her forehead. "Hardly a fool, Charlie. It was the one who published *Love, Death and Other Magicks.*"

As he left the kitchen, Charlie gripped the edge of the table, feeling distinctly unwell. It was too much, all at once, to have Ben going through so much, her father under so much pressure and then the discovery that her own success had brought it all about. She managed to put the cups and saucers in the sink before the tears started, then before she knew it, she was sobbing.

There was a knock at the kitchen door and she frantically wiped her eyes with the tea towel. She was still trying to compose herself when she heard the clip of smart shoes on the floorboards behind her.

"Miss Gunn? I was wondering if . . ." Magus Hopkins stopped when she turned to look at him. "May I help?"

She shook her head. "What can I do for you, Magus? Would you like some more tea?"

"No, thank you. Magus Ledbetter has left and Magus Ainsworth is speaking to your brother."

"Oh . . ." She tried not to look at him but that made her seem rude, so she grabbed the dishcloth and started wiping down the table instead. "Were you looking for my father?"

"Actually, I was hoping to speak to you."

That awful pounding grew stronger in her chest. "Papa knows much more about . . . about the timepiece, if that's what you're curious about."

He came closer and her industry increased until she was in danger of scrubbing a hole into the cloth. His hand, now free from its glove, reached over to touch the back of hers and stop her frantic work with the dishcloth. Another blush exploded across her cheeks at the contact and she froze. "Generally, Miss Gunn, when a Fellow of the Royal Society of the Esoteric Arts asks to speak with someone, it's considered more important than the cleanliness of a kitchen table."

Only two of his fingertips rested on the back of her hand with the lightest touch, yet it felt like the Magus had nailed her in place. Was he so forward with everyone? If George saw this now, he'd be incandescent. And yet the Magus didn't move away, didn't release her, until she finally looked into his eyes. "Whatever it is you fear, Miss Gunn, I'm sure it's not as bad as you believe. Perhaps if you were to ask me about your concerns, I could reassure you?"

At last, he moved his hand away and the breath came back into her chest in juddering snatches. Stalling for a few moments to try to regain some logical thought, Charlotte took the dishcloth back to the sink, rinsed it out and washed her hands. By the time she was drying them on the towel, she'd concluded that the magus wasn't going to leave without some sort of triumph. It was up to her to decide what form that would take.

"You seem very certain that I have concerns, even though I had the opportunity to ask questions earlier," she said, standing as far away from him as the small kitchen would allow.

"There were several people there, including your parents. From the way your brother looked at you, I suspect he knows what they are, but didn't want to say anything in front of them. I thought that an opportunity to speak to me in private would give you the freedom to ask whatever you wish, without fear of upsetting anyone."

It sounded reasonable enough, and Ben wasn't blessed with the best command of his facial expressions, but Charlotte couldn't shake the feeling that there was another reason behind the magus's interest. Regardless, she had to say something, if only to make him go away.

"How long will it be before Ben is allowed to come back home?"

Hopkins smirked. "You sound like someone asking when her brother will be allowed out of Newgate Gaol."

"How long, sir?"

"It varies. Some Latents take to the training very quickly and are safe in public within a matter of weeks. Others take a few months. No more than a year, though,

I'd wager. I haven't spoken to Benjamin yet, so I have no idea, but he seems bright enough."

"He's safe in public now," Charlotte said, the anger slipping out before she'd had a chance to smooth it over.

"But that would change."

"Really?"

"Surely you've heard about the accidents caused by those gone wild?"

Charlotte clenched her teeth, trying her best to keep her opinions trapped behind them. But the magus stared at her with those eyes and she felt like she was going to burst if she didn't say something. "There was a man at Speaker's Corner . . . he said that was all lies. He said that the Royal Society just traps gifted people and it's nothing more than slavery!"

His eyebrows shot up. "You think I am nothing more than a well-dressed slaver, come to take your brother from you?"

"No, sir, you would be a slave yourself, your views so moulded by your captors that you don't even realise what you are anymore, here to take my brother to make your owners pleased with you."

He stared at her, his expression unreadable.

"That's what the man at Speaker's Corner would say," she added.

"And what do you think, Miss Gunn?"

She'd said too much. This was exactly why she daren't risk being anything more than a secretive illustrator. Once she got upset about something, it pummelled her insides like a demon trapped within her, trying to escape. And then it always came out, at exactly the wrong time.

"I ... think I'm worried about my brother and I'm frightened that the man was right. He said so many things and they all made sense. But I can't ask anyone about it because if I do, they'll look at me as you are now."

"And these 'things' he said have been festering in your mind ever since. No wonder you seem so upset. About your brother."

He added the last three words a beat later. It was then that she noticed the trail of steam rising from the spout of the kettle, which had been pushed off the hot plate and rested at the back of the stove. She thought about the water inside, of it turning to ice, and the steam stopped. He didn't seem to have noticed it.

"I propose this, Miss Gunn," Hopkins said, leaning against the table, the luxurious dark brown brocade of his frock coat looking so out of place in their humble kitchen. "I will answer any question you have—no matter how dangerous or shocking it might be—and I will swear to you that those questions and the answers I give you will remain confidential. No one else need ever know."

She frowned at him. "Why are you so keen to ease *my* fears? Isn't it more important to make Ben feel comfortable?"

He smiled, and she hated the way it make her heart flip over and slap the inside of her chest, like a kipper being cooked in a pan. "It's painfully obvious that you and your brother are incredibly close. If he knows that you are happy, he will be happy. And a happy Latent does far better than an unhappy one. So, ask me a scandalous question and I will give you an honest answer."

"What happens to the people taken by the Enforcers?" At his intrigued expression, Charlotte added, "Ben and I saw a boy being taken from our local bakery this morning. It was rather distressing."

"Well, that's complicated," Hopkins began, and Charlotte could feel herself lowering her hopes of getting a decent answer. This man may be a magus, but he evidently still thought she should only hear a neat, oversimplified explanation, suitable for the feminine ear. "It depends how wild the Latent is, if they even are a Latent, why they've been hiding or as yet undiscovered and how motivated they are to hide their gift."

Charlotte gestured to one of the stools, her worries about receiving only a sanitised answer easing. "His mother didn't want to let him go, so I assume that's why it was being hidden, and the Enforcers often investigate a little before taking someone, otherwise it would be a lot of fuss wasted over false alarms," Charlotte reasoned out loud as she sat down. "So, let's say that boy is indeed 'gifted' and isn't yet wild; he's not even fourteen yet. He probably wants to go home to his mother, so let's assume he tries to hide his gift. What would happen to him?"

She could see that she'd narrowed the options to the one most difficult to discuss. Hopkins looked away to the window, eyes seeking something in his own reflection, perhaps. He was probably horribly vain. He sat down next to her. "There's a serious of tests, designed to force the unwilling Latent to manifest their ability. They are deeply unpleasant and I wouldn't wish the experience on anyone. The reluctant party is given many, many opportunities to cooperate before it reaches that point, but some people are . . . stubborn."

"Or frightened," she said, and he nodded.

"Yes, there have been a few who have grown up in families that have very . . . rigid religious beliefs and have convinced their child that any manifestation is a sign of Satan, rather than a gift from God. These poor souls often have the hardest transition into training."

"And no one is ever released if they don't want to be a magus?"

The skin between his eyebrows furrowed. "Of course not, Miss Gunn. As everyone knows, a Latent gone wild is incredibly dangerous. That we don't see that happen very often is a testament to the hard work of the Royal Society and the vigilance of the public. They must be trained, for the sake of everyone."

"And what if they refuse?"

He tilted his head. "I hardly think that is a concern that need be applied to your brother. He seems to be most willing, if a little nervous. Which is perfectly natural."

"You said you'd answer my questions."

Hopkins pursed his lips and smoothed his trousers over his knees. "Then they are incarcerated. And in the most extreme cases—where there is absolutely no other choice and they are too dangerous—they're executed."

It was Charlotte's turn to look out the window. She couldn't let him see her face, not when she was so afraid.

"But that is never going to happen to your brother, Miss Gunn. It's patently obvious that he is eager to test and will submit himself willingly. It's only those who continually refuse to accept what they are who are at risk. And they are given all the help it is in our power to give, to persuade them to become productive, valued Fellows of the Society."

Was that a euphemism for torture? If they locked her up in a dark cell, starved her, denied her contact with George and her family until she submitted to them, would that be called helping her?

She took a steadying breath and cleared her throat, but it still felt clogged. "And the magi cannot marry, is that correct?"

"That's correct."

"But what if they're in love?"

"Love is secondary to our duty to the Empire. Any love for an individual is nothing compared to our devotion to the Queen."

"But her soldiers in the army can marry! Her civil servants, her staff. Why not the magi?"

There was a pause, long enough to make her look at him again. He was staring at the floorboards and twisting a ring on his right hand. "It's forbidden in the Royal Charter, Miss Gunn. It was decided that enabling Fellows of the Royal Society to marry and bear children would create a conflict of interests for the magi involved. How could they devote their all to the Empire when they are devoted to—"

"Oh, what rot!" Charlotte exclaimed. "I'm sure that a general in the army feels no such conflict."

"But his wife is not being deployed to a battlefield, Miss Gunn. When we fight abroad, both men and women are on the field. What if a wife has to decide whether to send her husband or another, lesser magus to destroy an enemy battalion?"

"Favouritism must still be an issue in the regular army.

There's more to this than you're telling me."

Hopkins smiled at her. "You're far brighter than you let people see."

"You're avoiding answering my question," she replied, and he laughed. Strangely, she found she enjoyed the sound of it.

"I should imagine—remembering that this conversation is not to be shared—that it has far more to do with the risks that come with breeding hereditary lines. Whether the gift is passed in the blood remains a controversial topic; there is evidence both for and against. But there is no doubt that a family line which concentrates knowledge and resources for its own benefit above that of Queen and country would be inevitable, were marriage permitted."

"'. . . a family line which concentrates knowledge and resources . . .' That sounds more like a definition of nobility."

"You are too sharp for your own good, Miss Gunn. Now tell me, have I put your fears to rest?"

She considered his question. Some of her curiosity had been satisfied, but it had actually made her more afraid than before. She couldn't say anything to that effect, though. "I have one more question. You test at home, to make it more likely the Latent will perform well. But if that's the case, and Ben performs poorly once he leaves, will he be punished?"

Hopkins looked shocked at the suggestion. "Punished? We're not an institute of corrections, Miss Gunn. The Royal Society has far more in common with a university."

"Only compulsory," Charlotte added.

"Indeed, but aside from that, there are many similarities. All Latents manifest more easily in familiar environments before they're trained, so I expect there to be a significant drop in Benjamin's performance once he is recruited. Assuming he is, of course."

She nodded. "The evidence from the timepiece is irrefutable."

"Indeed. Now, I have a question for you, if I may?"

All the muscles in Charlotte's back tensed, but she couldn't refuse him, so she nodded.

"Your brother has been seriously ill on two occasions. Is there a chronic condition involved? Or two unrelated illnesses?" When she hesitated, he continued, "We need to know about such things in advance, Miss Gunn. We have the best physicians on call day and night." Another pause.. "It won't have any bearing on the compensation offered to your family. I give you my word."

Could she trust the word of a magus? Strange, all this time she'd been thinking of them as the faceless, masked terrors she'd seen dragging that boy into the carriage. But here she was, talking to one who seemed to be a reasonable person. Was she being lulled into dropping her defences because the way he looked was so distracting?

"In truth, sir, we don't know the cause of his illness. We could only afford to call the doctor once, and he suggested it was some sort of nervous disorder, given the symptoms and the timing of when he fell ill on both occasions." The fear bloomed in her chest that this mess they were in was going to cost Ben his life. "He's left home twice, to study, and both times he fell desperately ill. He gets feverish at first, then when that passes he just starts to waste away. It's awful. He only gets well when he comes home." Her eyes started to fill with tears again. "That's why I wanted to know how long he'll be locked up at the Royal Society."

"My dear lady, please stop speaking as if we are sending him to prison."

"It amounts to the same thing if he falls ill and can't return home."

He studied her face. "This has been a great strain on you. It must be very tiring, having to nurse him back to health."

"Exhausting," she confessed. "But seeing him get stronger every day keeps me going."

"He's very lucky to have such a devoted sister." He leaned in closer to her, making her lean back slightly. "Is that why you were so upset when I knocked on the door?"

He was so close, she could smell a sweet muskiness about him, a scent that made her want to move closer to him and breathe deeply. His eyes were fixed intently on hers, so striking they almost frightened her, as if a fundamental part of her soul could only accept someone so beautiful as being sent from another world to lure her into poor decisions. "That's . . . a very personal question, Magus Hopkins, and one I don't feel is particularly appropriate."

Expecting him to pull back, pushed away by the boundary she'd intended to remind him of, she waited. But he didn't move, didn't look away and didn't apologise. "I overheard the conversation with your father."

This time her blush was as much one of anger as of anything else. "Really, sir, you are too—"

"The place you mentioned, where lots of people die, you went there, didn't you?"

She made no effort to hide her surprise. "How did you know?"

"You sounded so certain, more certain than a woman told some numbers by a registrar's clerk."

"More than a mere clerk, sir—he's my fiancé!" Charlotte thrust her left hand in front of her. "Did you not notice the ring?"

Hopkins looked down on the gold band and its tiny sapphire, unimpressed. "You haven't denied it."

"I cannot fathom why you would have any interest if I did, sir. This is entirely unrelated to my brother's test."

"I had the impression this debt has everything to do with it. Your father said as much. Now, tell me, was this place in New Road, Whitechapel?"

A chill ran through her, deepening when he smiled. "I knew it!" he said. "And you're right to be worried about your father." He stood and pulled an exquisitely decorated timepiece from his pocket. "I should go back to the living room. I'm sure Ainsworth will be finished soon. Perhaps a cup of tea for your brother would be a good idea. He must be getting tired."

"Wait," she said as he made for the door. "You've heard of these debt collectors, too? Do you know anything about the cage in the back room?"

He stopped, evidently intrigued. "I don't, but I suspect I would like to. I can't go there myself, of course. A magus poking around in private business premises would not go down well, should I be discovered. If only I could call upon someone brave enough to examine it, but alas, that would be in breach of the rules controlling my influence."

She stood. "Are you trying to encourage me to go back there and break in?"

He looked so surprised, she even doubted herself. "Miss Gunn! The very idea! Oh, if you are planning to make a pot, I would be very grateful for a cup of tea, too.

Our conversation has made me quite thirsty." Hopkins opened the door and paused again, looking back at her. "It may interest you to know that the man you listened to on Speaker's Corner won't be there anymore. He's being prosecuted for slander."

She watched him leave, unable to stop her eyes drifting down to his calves, so shapely within the tight legs of his trousers. Shutting her eyes, Charlotte tried to work out whether that conversation had gone well and, more important, whether the magus had really been encouraging her to do something dangerous and most definitely unladylike.

Tea would help. She stood, stretched and went to get the kettle to fill it. It was only then that she noticed it was frosted and frozen solid to the stove. She could only hope that Hopkins was even less observant.

Chapter 8

THAT NIGHT, HOURS AFTER the consultations were over, Charlotte closed the back gate of number six, New Road. She leaned against it, hoping that no one had seen her. It was far too soon since the last time she'd felt this frightened, earlier that very day, when she was convinced the Enforcers were coming for her. Unlike then, however, she was finding this quite exhilarating.

She had never walked the streets of her local area alone at night, let alone sneaked into another area she barely knew that felt unsafe. She was wearing an old day dress that could be worn without a corset and crinoline cage, her old navy blue coat over the top and a black bonnet she had only ever worn once, to her aunt's funeral years before. Standing in the backyard of number six, New Road, she couldn't quite believe she was doing this.

It wasn't what she had planned to do; in fact, she'd tumbled into bed utterly exhausted only a couple of hours before, fully intending to sleep. Ben said the interviews had gone well, but he was so tired by the end of them that he'd done the same straight after supper, and her parents retired early, too. But no matter how much she needed to sleep, Charlotte couldn't settle. She'd fidgeted and fretted, going over the conversations she'd had with her father and with Magus Hopkins endlessly, picking over the details she could remember and worrying about those she could not.

The fact that thoughts of Magus Hopkins, of his lips in particular, plagued her was most disturbing. What was worse was that she hadn't realised her mind had slipped back to that place until she started to daydream about him leaning even closer when they'd been in the kitchen together. Appalled at herself, she thought of George and how sweet and kind he was, and twisted the engagement ring to remind herself she shouldn't be thinking of anyone else. It only worked for so long.

She soon discovered that the worry over her father and the debt collectors pushed any silliness from her mind. She wasn't convinced a polite letter from her father would make any difference, and the thought of him in that cage, dying from a heart attack, made her sit up and light the candle again.

Why did Magus Hopkins know about that house in particular? Had he owed money to them before he became a Fellow of the Royal Society? Did he know others who had fallen afoul of Anchor Financial Services? Whatever the reason for his interest, he'd made it clear that he wasn't prepared to find out more.

But there was nothing stopping her from doing that.

So now she stood at the back of the dark house, using the moonlight to pick out the back door handle and the window. She couldn't see into the room she'd looked at before, and with it being so dark, she wasn't sure if it was because the house was empty or if thick curtains had been drawn and were blocking out any light.

Tiptoeing across the backyard, she jumped when the clock towers across the city chimed midnight. They wouldn't chime again until six o'clock the next day, and she hoped desperately that when they did, she'd be asleep in her own bed, safe once more.

Charlotte pressed her ear to the back door and then to the ground floor window, listening for any sound coming from within. She couldn't hear anything, but with two dogs barking in nearby streets and the background rumble of carriage wheels on cobbles and trains in the distance, she wasn't confident in her appraisal. Cupping her hands around her eyes again, she pressed against the bottom left corner of the window and was heartened to see a sliver of moonlight stretching across the floor inside. Whilst it made the cage loom out of the shadows like something out of a nightmare, it was reassuring to see that the room was empty.

She tried the handle on the back door and, as she expected, it was locked. She returned to the window and looked for the clasp keeping the lower sash locked in place. When Charlotte saw that it was just like the ones they had at home, with a simple curved bolt to slide out with one small movement, she smiled. She knew how they felt, where the resistance would be and where the force needed to be applied to open it.

Crouching down until her eyes were level with the lock on the other side of the glass, and trying not to think too much about the awful things her dress was being dragged through, Charlotte shifted from side to side until the moonlight shone on as much of the lock as possible. Then she imagined her hand being able to pass through the window frame to press her thumb against the flattened edge of the hasp, pushing it sideways to slide the rest of the semicircle out.

At first, she feared it wasn't going to work, and then all of a sudden the lock swung round so fast she squeaked in surprise. She shrank lower in the shadows as another dog started to bark, sounding much closer than the others. What would her mother say if she knew what Charlotte were doing now? Even worse, what would George think? He simply wouldn't believe it. Then she caught herself wondering how Magus Hopkins would react and couldn't stop herself mirroring the smile she fancied would spread on those lips of his.

"Charlotte Persephone Gunn, you should be ashamed of yourself!" she whispered to her own shadow, but not because she was about to break into a private property.

The window was mercifully easy to open, and she climbed in over the windowsill. She could only hope that no one had been looking out of the many darkened windows that overlooked the back of the house and its grubby yard. After pausing to listen carefully again, she pulled the lower sash back down but left it open just a crack for peace of mind. The house was silent and somehow felt empty. The air was surprisingly stale, considering that man who had been in there earlier, and it smelt of damp walls. She could imagine the mould creeping up the walls and the size of the spiders in the shadows and was glad she could see neither.

She could see very little, in fact. The moonlight only stretched so far in and barely reached the edge of the cage. Charlotte had planned ahead, though—she could list her many failings, but being unprepared was rarely one of them. She fetched a candle and holder from the old leather satchel worn beneath her coat, and after taking a moment to drag the heavy drapes across the window, she lit the candle with barely an afterthought. It took her a moment to regulate the flame she'd created at the tip of the wick, then she shifted her attention to the room again.

The candlelight threw more shadows than it gave comfort, but at least she could inspect things more closely. First, she went to the open doorway to the rest of the house and saw a front parlour that was little more than a small reception room–cum–office. There was a cabinet of the sort that contained paperwork, a dusty desk and chair tucked beneath it and a couple of rickety wooden chairs on the other side of it. There was just enough light from the candle to show several locks on the inside of the front door and a blind pulled down in the front window. At least none of the neighbours across the street would be able to see inside. She saw a letter on the floor next to the front door. From the extravagant loops on the handwriting, she suspected it was the one her father said he would send. It must have arrived in the second post.

Bare wooden stairs rose up to her left, and she had the sudden, awful thought that the proprietor could be asleep in a room up there. Expecting that horrible broom-moustached man to come clattering down in long johns any moment, Charlotte retreated back to the room she was interested in, planning to see as much as she could as quickly as possible. As she turned to go back to where she'd entered, she thought she saw a man out of the corner of her eye, tall and slender, staring at the cage. She jolted, making the candle wobble in the holder, and then realised there was no one there. Her fears were getting the better of her.

Charlotte retraced her steps, taking care to keep her heels off the floorboards. It was cold in the room, cold enough for her to see her breath, and there was no fireplace that she could see. There were marks on the wall where there was once a stove similar to the one at home and in the corner an area was curtained off behind grey cotton that was once white. Her imagination swiftly placed a man behind it, waiting to jump out at her, so she headed straight for it and pulled the curtain back. She found nothing more than a filthy sink with a cluster of old tin mugs nestled in it, covered in spider webs.

Relieved, she let the curtain drop back into place and approached the cage. It must have been where all those poor souls died. *Cage* didn't seem an adequate word as she approached it. It was too sturdy, too imposing, more like a prison cell, but freestanding in the centre of the room. It was large enough to hold a tall man if he stood but not if he lay down, being only four feet square by her estimate. It must have been assembled in the room, being too large to fit through doorway or window, with a solid iron base and top into which the thick bars were slotted.

As she approached, Charlotte couldn't help but shudder. It felt like the time George took her to see the waxworks at the Baker Street Bazaar and they had braved the separate room in which the re-created scenes of violence from the French Revolution had made her feel faint. There was no blood, nothing but iron in fact, but something of that horror lingered here. The promise of cruelty, perhaps, or simply the reminder of how one person could so easily abuse and debase another. The draught from the open window caught wisps of her hair that tickled the back of her neck, and she clenched her teeth tight together to stop them chattering. There was such a sense of death here, such a feeling of despair. The thought of anyone, let alone her father, being subjected to imprisonment here was enough to make her want to weep.

The candle flame flickered and then, as she watched it, it curved to the right—against the direction of the draught from the window—in such an unnatural manner that for a moment, she wondered if she were somehow doing it herself. After convincing herself that she was not, she moved the candle holder slowly in a circle, studying the way the flame reminded her of a compass needle, remaining pointed in its chosen direction.

Charlotte lifted the candle in the direction the flame pointed until she saw a mark on the slab of iron that formed the roof of the cage, where the flame straightened again. There was something engraved or stamped into the iron, like a hallmark, only larger. It was a rectangular shape the size of her thumbnail, filled with several symbols that overlapped in places.

The flame tugged sharply to the left and she saw another at the other end of the metal edge. A quick circuit of the cage confirmed that the same hallmark was stamped into the iron at each of the corners, on the lid and base. An inspection of the bars revealed a different symbol, simpler in design, set into an oval that was half the size of the others and stamped into each bar at the top and bottom.

This was important. She knew it. It didn't seem like a manufacturer's mark—there would only be the need for one, after all. Her instinct was that it had something to do with magic, though how the marks could influence the candle flame, she had no idea. As far as she knew, a magus had to be present to do anything like that.

Whatever they were, she couldn't stand there staring at them all night. She set the candle down, fished out her small notebook and pencil and copied both of the "hallmarks" down as accurately as she could. Just as she was finishing the second, smaller design, she heard the sound of a key tumbling a lock in the front door.

She dropped the pencil in her panic, scrabbled to find where it had rolled to as the second lock was tumbled, grabbed it and the candle holder as the third lock was opened and darted behind the curtain as a start was made on the fourth. Charlotte licked her fingertips and pinched out the candle flame, freezing the wick to choke off the smoke's distinctive scent. Then she remembered, with heart-stopping horror, that she'd left the curtains closed and window open. Leaving the satchel and candle behind the curtain, she just had time to dash across, set everything back as quietly as she could to how it had been when she arrived and then race back to the curtained nook as the last lock was opened.

Pressing herself back against the sink in an effort to keep her toes away from the curtain, Charlotte tried not to think of the spiders that might be crawling up her coat, into her hair, as the sound of two sets of footfalls echoed from the office area. She could smell the dank air rising up from the drain beneath the plughole and hoped desperately that she wouldn't catch something awful from the miasma.

"I told ya, every time there's one on the way, he wants it checked," a gruff male voice said.

"But the last one was only last week," said a different male voice that she'd heard somewhere before. "'Ent that much could 'appen since then. No one's been 'ere."

"Them's the rules," said the first. They both spoke with London accents, but the second was deeper and vaguely familiar.

Both men entered the room with the cage, one of them carrying a lantern. Its light stretched beneath the shabby curtain, making Charlotte stand on tiptoe so she could move her feet just a couple of inches further back into the shadows. The light penetrated the thin fabric and Charlotte was certain that any moment they would spot her, as she could see their silhouettes on the other side. She could only hope that her own blended sufficiently against the outline of the sink in a forgotten corner. But what if one of them decided they wanted a drink of water? A burning rush up from her stomach made her swallow several times as she told herself that no one would ever want to use one of the foul mugs resting behind her.

"So, then," said the familiar voice, "what's it like, now you're one of them?"

"I was always one of 'em. I just got a fancy bit of paper and me own mark now."

"Let's see it, then."

"No, it's private."

"What, they tattoo it on or summat?"

"Course they don't. Hold this."

Charlotte watched the bright core of the lantern light swing over to the left as the unfamiliar man handed it to the second to hold. There was the sound of keys jangling and then the clunk of one of them being put into a lock, presumably the one in the cage door.

"You were always a lucky little sod," said the voice she couldn't place. "If only all my sons were magi. I'd be too bleeding rich to get up to this sort of bizniss."

"Don't be so ungrateful, Pa. You've never 'ad it so good. You don't have to live in this dive anymore for one thing, thanks to me."

"Thanks to your guvnor, more like. What's he really like?"

"How he seems," the son said, and the sound of his boots changed to a soft clank as he presumably climbed inside the cage. "That's what I like about 'im. He seems like a bullying old bastard and that's exactly what he is. You know where you are with 'im. If he's angry, you know it, it hurts, then it's over. Job done. Move on."

Why was he getting inside the cage? Charlotte tried to wrestle her curiosity down deep inside, make it smaller, quieter, but it was too much. She parted the curtain opening just enough to give her a sliver to spy out of, and bit her lip when she recognised the man holding the lantern. He was the one who'd delivered the letter to her father. He was holding a letter again, now, in the hand not holding up the lantern. The one she suspected was from her father. He must have picked it up when they came in.

His son was inside the cage, with the door still open, kneeling down as she watched. He rummaged in a pocket and then pulled out a screwdriver.

"What kind of a magus are you, needin' one of those?" his father scoffed. "Thought you could do all that with the power of your thoughts, like them mesmerists."

"It's nothing like mesmerism," said the son, directing the tool at something in the base of the cell that Charlotte couldn't see before starting to unscrew. "And I'm not that type of magus. Can't do the fiddly stuff like this."

"Nah, you never were one for delicate fings," said the father, setting the lantern down next to where his son worked. He opened the letter, chuckled to himself and then stuffed it in a pocket.

"Who's that from?"

"The bloke who'll be in here on Friday. Beggin' for more time. They always do. Silly sod should 'ave lived within 'is means. Now he owes twice as much and is spinning some bollocks about his son testin' to be one of you lot."

The son paused, looked up. "They'll pay 'im, if he is."

"Don't make no difference to me, son. I reckon your guvnor wouldn't be impressed if I told 'im this one got off the 'ook. And anyway, what he'll pay me is far more than what this pillock's debt is. In for the long term, me."

Charlotte had never hated anyone so intensely as she hated that man now. The fury and disgust erupted inside her and the flame in the lantern brightened sharply before she got a proper grip on it all and pressed it down. Losing her temper now was not going to help her father, or bring justice to this despicable man. It would only get her killed.

"Last one," the son said as he attacked another screw, as if he and his father were chatting about something as harmless as fishing.

Scowling at the son, Charlotte did all she could to memorise his features. He had the same bushy sort of moustache as his father, though slightly better groomed, a long, thin face with a narrow mouth and close-set eyes. She would have no trouble remembering him. Surely the Royal Society of Esoteric Arts would be very interested to know that one of their recently installed fellows was involved in some sort of bizarre . . . what, exactly?

The last screw removed, the magus dropped the screwdriver back into his pocket, lifted a plate of metal that was a half yard square and rested it against the inside of the nearest bars. He reached down inside—further than the depth of the cell base, presumably through a hole in the floorboards beneath?—and with a grunt, he lifted something up until it clunked into place and remained elevated without his effort.

It was unlike anything Charlotte had ever seen before. A mechanism of some kind, reminiscent of the internal workings of the timepiece she'd sketched, but with fewer cogs and more vials of liquid, connected to each other in a complex array of copper and lead piping. There was a central dial that the magus examined, marked at intervals with symbols too small for her to see properly and some sort of ratchet that held it in a particular position.

"See, told ya it were all where it should be."

"I still have to check, Pa. This stuff is dangerous."

"Don't I know it, son! I'm the poor bugger who 'as to come in here with that doctor when 'e signs 'em off."

Knowing that this was something desperately important, Charlotte committed as much of the mechanism to memory as possible. She wanted to sketch it then and there, but was too afraid they'd hear her rooting about in her satchel for the notebook and pencil. So she stayed as still as she could, noting all the tiny details, closing her eyes for a second to visualise it and then opening them again to fill in the parts that were hazy in her memory. By the time the son had satisfied himself that whatever that dread machine did was still in working order, she was confident she could remember it.

"When's the next one in?" the magus asked.

"That's the Friday one who wrote the letter. Got some others on the boil, but they've got a bit more time." The man lowered his voice, as though he was fearful of being overheard. "Listen . . . you can tell your old man. What's all this for?"

"I told yer, Pa, I can't say."

"That thing . . . that magical stuff . . . It's what makes their tickers stop, innit?"

The magus didn't answer, but Charlotte knew it was

true. The numbers didn't lie, as George had told her several times, and far too many people died here for it to be coincidence. Whilst he attributed it to stress, now she'd seen the device, she knew foul play was at work. But why? It obviously had some purpose other than killing people. What could it be?

Charlotte withdrew from the gap in the curtain, letting it fall shut when the magus replaced the metal lid after dropping the machine back into place. She held her breath as the cell was closed again and the two men left the room. It wasn't until she heard their footsteps leave the house, the slam of the front door behind them, and the turning of the locks once more that she allowed herself a moment to sag and draw in several deep, steadying breaths.

After waiting a few minutes, just to be certain they had truly left, Charlotte left the foul cubby and lit the candle once more. She sketched the mechanism then and there, kneeling on the floorboards whilst it was fresh in her mind, followed by a quick sketch of the magus, before taking one last look at the cell.

Charlotte didn't know how, but she was going to put a stop to this. Not just for her father, but for all the other poor souls these evil men would target in the future. She tucked the notebook and pencil away, blew out the candle and headed for the window. It was time for this rude young woman to make a difference.

Chapter 9

ON THE WAY TO New Road earlier that night, Charlotte had looked over her shoulder every minute or so and glanced fearfully at dark windows, scared that some unsavoury creature would spot a young woman out alone and pursue her. The bark of a dog or the slamming of a door had been enough to make her jolt and sometimes almost stumble into the gutter in her nervousness.

The way back from New Road felt so very different. She was too angry to be afraid of imaginary threats in the shadows. The Royal Society crowed about how they kept everyone safe, how they regulated the use of magic to ensure the good citizens of the Empire were never at risk. And now she had firm evidence that one of their order—no, two!—were involved in the deaths of so many misfortunate people, damned because they had borrowed money and been unable to pay it back.

She'd report all she'd discovered to the local magistrate first. George had told her he was a decent chap and all she needed to do was show him what she'd found and tell him about the cluster of deaths.

But magi were involved. Should she instead go to Master Judicant with her discovery? His job was to see things done properly and fairly wherever the magi were involved. And he would be impartial whereas the magistrate—

She collided with a man who stepped out of nowhere. Charlotte was so lost in her furious planning that it knocked her over. She banged her head on the pavement and cried out, more in surprise than pain, then realised a gloved hand was reaching down to help her up.

"I'm so dreadfully sorry, miss, it was my fault. Oh, Miss Gunn! What a surprise!"

Charlotte blinked away the momentary dizziness to focus on Magus Hopkins, dressed in white tie, top hat and evening cloak. She felt dreadfully underdressed as he pulled her to her feet. "Magus Hopkins? What in heaven's name are you doing here?"

"Walking back from a soiree." He looked her up and down, noticing the absence of crinoline, no doubt. "I might ask the same of you. Do your parents know you're stalking the streets of Whitechapel in the small hours of the morning?"

"Hardly 'stalking,' sir."

Too ashamed to look at him dressed as she was, Charlotte brushed her coat off instead.

"What's this?"

She looked up to see Hopkins picking up her notebook, which must have fallen from her satchel. He opened it and flipped through, looking at the sketches beneath the pool of gaslight from the lamppost.

"That's mine!" She rushed over and tried to grab it, but he turned as if he were in a waltz with her, keeping the notebook out of reach.

"Well, this is very interesting," he muttered at the last pages. "Where did you sketch these, Miss Gunn?"

"That is none of your business, sir."

"Oh, but I think it is. This is a contraption with an esoteric purpose, and a terribly dangerous one, by all appearances. That's assuming that this drawing is accurate."

"Indeed it is, sir!"

"So you saw it with your own eyes, did you?"

Charlotte clenched her fists. Why, of all the people in London, did this awful man have to bump into her right now?

Hopkins looked back at the sketch. "Very interesting indeed. Of course"—he pulled a pencil of his own from inside his tailcoat breast pocket—"it would be rendered utterly harmless should this dial be changed to this setting here, and the pin that holds that ratchet was repositioned to . . . here . . ." He drew little arrows to illustrate his comments. He stopped and looked wickedly mischievous, just for a moment, before smiling at her and tucking the pencil back in its place. "But I forget myself in my fondness for delicate mechanisms. I shouldn't speculate about such matters in the presence of the uninitiated. Which brings me back to my question. Did you see this? No, that much is obvious. Where did you see it?"

She reached for the notebook again and he held it out of her reach, pulling it away in the last moment so she stepped close enough to him to smell his scent again. He tilted his face towards her, now closer than they had been in the kitchen. Charlotte's rage, briefly knocked out of her with the air in her lungs, sprung back with a fearsome burst. How dare he toy with her! She stamped on his foot and he cried out, dropping the notebook, which she retrieved triumphantly and stuffed into her satchel. She buckled it tightly shut as he hobbled to lean against the lamppost. "Oh, I'm so sorry, Magus Hopkins. Did I tread on your toes? I do beg your pardon."

He scowled at her, and then threw his head back and laughed so heartily that she had to fight the smile that threatened her own face. "Miss Gunn, it is I who should apologise. Let us begin again. Please, will you permit me to escort you home? These really aren't the streets a decent young woman should walk alone at night."

Charlotte couldn't help but agree with his appraisal. "Thank you. I'd like you to escort me to wherever I might find Master Judicant, if you'd be so kind, sir."

Hopkins frowned. "Is this regarding the sketch I saw in your notebook?"

Whilst she was fairly certain he wasn't involved, given his encouragement to look into the property at New Road, Magus Hopkins was still a Fellow of the Royal Society and so she had to tread carefully. But the connection between the sketch and her desire to see Master Judicant was so obvious, she would seem foolish to deny it. "It is. And I don't wish to be rude, sir, but I cannot discuss this with you, being a Fellow of the Royal Society yourself."

He adjusted his hat, patting it back into place after his exertions and extended his arm to her. She hesitated, wondering if it would be appropriate to accept. "I think any patrolling Peelers are far less likely to question my motives if we walk thus, Miss Gunn. And I assure you I have no inappropriate intentions towards you, especially as you are engaged to be married."

She tucked her hand into the crook of his arm and decided that if she didn't walk as close to him as she did George, her conscience would be clear. "Do you know where to find him?"

They started walking. A carriage went past, then another. Charlotte looked at the magus, waiting for the answer. "Miss Gunn, I beg you to consider how it would appear if you went to Master Judicant with the drawing you have and . . . perhaps I'm being presumptuous . . . some rather serious allegations against a Fellow of the Royal Society." When she didn't deny it, he continued, "You are a young woman from a respectable household, granted, but your brother is currently going through the process of being tested."

"My brother has absolutely nothing to do with this!"

"Gosh, you are so very protective of him, aren't you? My dear Miss Gunn, I disagree. There is ample evidence already to suggest he is a Latent, and I am fairly certain that by the end of tomorrow he will have proven his potential. Imagine that you lodge a complaint against the Society at exactly the same time he is recruited. Don't you think that could make things difficult for him?"

Charlotte frowned at the pavement. "It shouldn't. He has done nothing wrong. It's my duty to report what I've discovered! I cannot stay silent when people's lives are at risk. Besides, surely Master Judicant will root out the evil within the Royal Society and the rest will be grateful that this has been exposed."

"When what has been exposed?"

"Murder!"

As soon as she said it, Charlotte knew she'd made a mistake. His grip on her hand tightened in the crook of his arm and he stopped, forcing her to do so, too. "Miss Gunn, I am about to offer you some advice that you will not want to accept. I beg you to listen to me and even when you want to argue against it, to listen anyway. You must not go to Master Judicant and make these accusations."

"But—"

"If you were to go there now, he would no doubt listen to you and he may believe you. You have formed a good impression upon him. But then should anything further escalate from your actions, you and your family will be at terrible risk. The Royal Society will close ranks and will seek to destroy your reputation. They will ask how you came to have such a drawing. I presume you were not shown this, but instead obtained the intelligence by . . . unorthodox means? Breaking and entering, perhaps?"

Charlotte's cheeks burned and he nodded, satisfied. "But it should not matter, sir! What matters more is that people are dying and it has something to do with that mechanism, I know it! There's some sort of . . . of—"

"Conspiracy?" he asked, gently. "My dear lady, there have been dozens of accusations of conspiracy levelled against the Royal Society over the years. Do you know how many have actually resulted in a prosecution?" At the shake of her head, he said, "None. Precisely zero. Even if you managed to make enough people believe you to investigate your claims, nothing, save the destruction of your reputation and most probably worse, will come of it."

She turned to look at him properly, examining his face for any sign of deception. All she saw were sadness and concern. She could hardly trust her appraisal, though, for even now she couldn't help but be swayed by his beauty. Was he telling the truth or merely trying to protect his own? She couldn't remember any news about accusations against the Society; in fact, that was why she had been so interested in the man at Speaker's Corner. No one ever said or printed anything like what he said. Now he was being prosecuted, rather than the Royal Society, as he had been insisting should happen.

Then the futility of her position hit her. As tears welled, she realised there was nothing to be done about evil people with the wealth, power and influence that a fellowship of the Royal Society bestowed upon them. She was nothing, a girl who secretly earned a paltry amount of money compared to theirs, waiting to marry a sensible man and be one of the millions trying to make a decent life in this harsh, unforgiving city. She had to hide what made her special, be it her artistic talent or the burden of her magical affinity, and neither could serve her here.

"But my father," she whispered, looking down as the first tear broke free. "I must do something, or he will die! And others after him."

What was she doing, standing on a street corner with

a magus she barely knew, weeping in front of him? This simply wouldn't do. She sniffed and tried to find a handkerchief, oscillating between despair and frustration. "If I can't act," she said, giving up on her search and using the back of her hand to wipe the tear away, "can't you? You already suspect—"

"I've said far too much already," Hopkins declared, starting off again and pulling her with him. "I think it's best that we speak of something else, in fact. Tell me about your fiancé."

"No. You knew the house I spoke of this afternoon was in New Road. You have suspicions, you can't deny that."

"Do you have a date for the wedding?" he asked cheerily, as if they were chatting over a cup of tea and a bun in some tearoom. "Waiting for the spring, perhaps? A spring wedding is such a delight, after all."

"Stop mocking me, sir! I'm not some simpleton, happy to be distracted by talk of weddings and happy endings! I am talking about my father's life and I am begging you for help!"

He stayed maddeningly silent, doing nothing except closing his left hand over hers in the crook of his elbow. When she tried to pull away, he held her hand tightly and practically marched her along the street. She looked for a Peeler, for anyone, but the street was empty save a stray dog sniffing in the gutter ahead.

"I understand the concern you have for your father, Miss Gunn," he finally said, just as she was about to call out for help. "But I beg you to consider the fate of your brother."

"Are you threatening—"

"No," he said sharply. "Nothing of the sort. But if you act openly against any Fellow of the Society on the brink of your brother's training, you will do nothing but encourage your enemy's allies to make his life a misery. I do not envy your position, Miss Gunn, and I am not without sympathy. But I will not, I *cannot*, act against my fellow magi."

They were only one street away from home now. She stopped pulling at her hand, allowing him to guide them across the road, hoping she could persuade him. "You refuse to act, even though people are being murdered?"

"There's something you need to understand," Hopkins said. "I am just as powerless as you are, Miss Gunn. You probably think me a despicable chap, unwilling to assist a helpless young lady in distress. And in some respects, I am. But you are not a helpless young lady. You are more resourceful than you want anyone to believe. Perhaps you have forgotten that. Perhaps you have started to believe your own lie about yourself. Either way, I urge you to consider what you can achieve, rather than what I refuse to do."

He stopped and she realised they'd reached the end of her road. He released her hand long enough for him to clasp hold of it and press his lips to her skin. The breath caught in her chest as he looked up at her, his lips still pressed against her hand for a moment that seemed to last far longer. She could only breathe again when he released her. Her toes were aching.

"I bid you good night, Miss Gunn. I will see you in the morning. May I suggest you remain at home, until then?"

She backed away and then ran to her house, desperate to get away from the way he made her feel. How could she be so furious with someone and yet so disarmed by a single kiss? Urgh! She hated herself almost as much as she hated him and his refusal to help. What a cowardly man, knowing what he did and refusing to do a single thing—

She stopped at the bottom of the steps, remembering what he had said when he first looked at the sketch of the mechanism. She was such a fool! She'd been so distressed by the fact that he'd seen it, that she hadn't fully taken in what he was doing in. She unbuckled the satchel, pulled out the notebook and checked the drawing. There were the arrows he'd drawn! Whilst he was unwilling to expose what was happening, Magus Hopkins had given her a way to "render it harmless." It would be enough to help her father in the short term whilst she worked out the best way to bring those men to justice without harming her brother.

Smiling, she looked for the magus at the end of the street, but he'd already gone. She was tempted to go back to the cage now, get it over with, but from what the men had said, it wouldn't be in use until Friday. She had another night to go back and alter it, and she had to get some rest now. Tricking the magi was going to take all the energy she could muster; otherwise, her family's fortunes were never going to change.

Chapter 10

THE NEXT MORNING, everyone was up bright and early, or rather just early in Charlotte's case. If it weren't for her nerves about the day ahead, she was sure she could have slept for hours longer.

Poor Ben hardly touched his breakfast, despite everyone's best efforts to encourage him to keep his strength up. "I'm so dreadfully nervous," he confessed to Charlotte as they both went upstairs afterwards.

She followed him into his room and closed the door behind them. "I'll be with you the whole time," she said. "Not in the room, obviously, but close enough to help. Just try your hardest at the tasks they want you to do and try not to look too surprised if they go very well."

"Are you sure about this, Charlie? Isn't this horribly dishonest?"

She thought of the cell, of the Enforcers dragging that poor baker's son from his mother and what Magus Hopkins had said about the way the Royal Society closed ranks against anyone who questioned it. She simply couldn't muster any sense of guilt about what she was planning. "This is going to change your life forever. I would much rather we keep you and not see a penny of their money, but we don't have that choice, so we may as well do all we can to make sure Mother and Father are financially secure. Making sure we're well compensated is not dishonest."

"But I do feel that we're trying to pass off a paste gem as a diamond."

Charlotte shook her head. "It's not like that at all! You *are* a diamond. You just haven't had all the facets cut yet."

"But you're going to make them think I'm far more able than I am. What happens when I am by myself and I can barely alter a candle flame?"

Whilst it was an understandable fear, it saddened her to see Ben so lacking in self-belief. "Magus Hopkins said there's always a drop in performance between testing and starting training. Don't worry about a thing."

Ben tugged at his shirt sleeve, trying and failing to make the fashionable amount extend beyond his jacket cuff. It was slightly too small. "What if I pass the test, start my training and fall ill again?"

It was a fear she shared, but they were past the point of changing anything now. There was a sharp pang of guilt that she hadn't put herself forward instead of him. Was it too late? "Ben, if you don't want to do this, I'll tell them the truth. Your health means far more to me than—"

He embraced her. "No, dear heart. I know you don't want to step forward, and I won't force you. You've spent your whole life looking after me, nursing me, even funding me, to my shame. This is my only chance to help the family. I have to take it!"

"I'll never forgive myself if anything—"

"Shush." He held her tighter. "I've been thinking about this. Perhaps . . . perhaps I fell ill both times because somehow, deep down, my body knew I was following the wrong path. Perhaps if I learn to be all I can be, reach my potential, perhaps then I will be healthy."

It sounded so desperate and so unlikely, but Charlotte allowed herself to be released from the embrace so she could smile and nod at him. "That makes a great deal of sense. Yes. In a matter of months we shall take tea together, you a magus, me a happily married woman, and we shall laugh about how frightened we were today."

She left him to prepare himself, and after helping her mother to sweep the living room and dining room and beat the hallway rug, she retired to her bedroom to tidy herself up before the magi and Master Judicant arrived. She put on one of her best dresses and neatened her hair. She pinched her cheeks as she stood in front of the looking glass, trying to bring some colour back into her face. The dark shadows beneath her eyes made her sigh. Magus Hopkins must think her such a plain creature indeed.

Her hand flew to her mouth. Why should she care what he thought of her?

She wished George were free that evening. She was eager to tell him what had happened since her visit to his office. The safe parts, at least.

But now was not the time to think about either of them. She went to the wooden chest, lifted out the linens of her trousseau, moved her sketchbook and pencils aside and pulled out the shoe box filled with letters from George and souvenirs of their outings together. She paused when she opened it and saw a silhouette of him that had been cut by a man in the park for a ha'penny. It made her smile before she reached beneath it and the other ticket stubs and letters to find the small pair of opera glasses hidden beneath.

Strange to think that she had been so disappointed when she'd received them as a gift. Her agent had sent them to her and luckily they had arrived when her parents were otherwise engaged. The glasses were a gift from a rather eccentric author for whom she had illustrated a book on theatre costumes, based on several that had been sent to her agent's office. "For you to enjoy the details you so artfully illustrate whilst in situ," the note had read. She had tried them out once by looking out of her window and then wrapped them back up in the tissue paper they'd arrived in. What use had she for such a frivolous item? When would she ever go to a theatre and be able to sit in one of the expensive seats that merited the use of opera glasses?

Now she could have kissed that strange author.

She knelt down, spent a few moments wrestling her crinoline cage into a position that was mostly not in the way and rolled back the thin rug that ran down the side of her bed. With practically all her father's income spent on rent over the years, and her mother's modest seamstress income spent on food and other essentials, the furnishings that had been passed down in the family had never been replaced and were rather worse for wear. The minor repairs that the landlord refused to see to and that her father couldn't afford to fix were still there, too, including the loose floorboard that was currently held in place by a couple of loose nails that had to be beaten back into place with a shoe every once in a while.

She winkled them out with her fingertips and then lifted it up to reveal the rafters below, right above where an old plaster ceiling rose was positioned. It was a leftover from the time when the four houses in their row were actually part of one large Georgian manor house. When the manor was sold and converted to separate, smaller dwellings with gas lighting, the old central chandelier was removed but the ceiling rose remained. It was a swirling, leafy and elaborate rococo design with lots of gaps between the plaster flowers, through which she could see the room below.

She'd discovered it as a child, soon after they'd moved in, and had used it to spy upon her mother sewing and her father illustrating. So many of the things she went on to practise and perfect herself were inspired by what she'd seen him draw below, when her parents thought she was asleep. Now she was counting on the same spy holes to enable her to help Ben impress the magi.

After placing everything back in the wooden chest, hiding the opera glasses beneath her pillow and replacing the floorboard without the nails, there was nothing to do but wait.

Like the day before, Master Judicant arrived first and inspected the dining room. He asked that her mother's sewing box be removed, along with her father's chest of paper and art supplies, which needed to be partially emptied before he could carry it out. It was all to do with minimising risk, apparently, and Charlotte was glad precautions were being taken. All the while, Ben rested upstairs, marshalling his strength for the trials ahead. Charlotte wished she could do the same.

Each of the magi who had visited the day before had a scheduled time to come to test Ben, with Magus Ainsworth first on the list. She arrived just before nine o'clock, carrying a small black leather case, and after a polite round of good mornings, Master Judicant ushered her and Ben into the dining room.

"Do you mind if I rest whilst the test is happening, Mother?" Charlotte asked. "I'm so tired. I hardly slept."

"Of course," Mother said, kissing her on the forehead. "You've been an angel. Your father and I will be in the living room if you need us."

Charlotte climbed the stairs, watching Father put an arm around Mother and kiss her cheek in an effort to reassure her. They both looked equally nervous.

Soon Charlotte was kneeling in place over the spy holes, opera glasses in her hand, ear level with the remaining floorboards as she listened in.

"Well, now," said Magus Ainsworth, "as I explained yesterday, I'm going to ask you to do some things that a Latent may find difficult, but a non-gifted will find impossible. I don't want you to worry about how hard it is, or if it takes you a little while to complete each task. What matters is that you try your best."

Magus Ainsworth put the leather case on the table. It had an unusually ornate clasp that had been enamelled in several bright colours, but was otherwise the same as any other Charlotte had seen. The magus opened it and took out a wooden case, opening that to reveal a velvet-lined interior holding a large candle, similar to those Charlotte had seen in church. She handed it to Master Judicant, who inspected it carefully with sight and touch, from the tip of the wick to the base. After a nod, he handed back to Ainsworth, who put it on the table in front of Ben after pushing the box and the case to one side.

"We talked yesterday about how my specialism deals with temperature. Raising it, lowering it, regulating it. You might have heard of how the thermatological arts are involved in the production of iron and steel, but there are many other applications you'll learn of, should you choose the college I represent. Now"—she stood—"I'm going to leave this room, but I will be nearby, should I be needed. Whilst I'm gone, I'd like you to ignite the wick without the use of any tools or assistance of any kind. You're not permitted to touch the candle, but you may look at it. Do you understand the task?"

Ben nodded. "Yes, ma'am."

"Good luck, young man," Ainsworth said, and after giving Master Judicant a courteous nod, she left the room.

"In your own time, Latent," Master Judicant said after he'd moved the position of the candle.

Charlotte shifted so the wick was in sight, just a few metres away. All she had to do was calm herself down and—

"Charlotte?" Her mother was coming up the stairs!

She got to her feet, glad she'd had the sense to take off

her shoes, and the floorboard creaked. She froze, wondering whether it would make Master Judicant suspect foul play, but then heard her mother approaching her room. Hurriedly she grabbed the rug and laid it over the gap as quietly as she could and tiptoed to the door.

Her mother knocked once and then opened it, just as Charlotte was reaching for the handle. Her mother frowned at the way her skirt hung in disarray over the crinoline cage. Charlotte hurriedly smoothed the material. "I was lying down."

"You're not unwell, are you?" Poor Mother. Any sign of the slightest illness in her children alarmed her so much.

"Only a slight headache. Did you need me?"

"Father offered to go to the bakery. Would you like a currant bun to have with elevenses? We thought it might be a nice treat for Ben."

It took everything in Charlotte's self-control repertoire not to seem impatient. How was her mother to know Ben needed her right now? "A currant bun would be lovely, thank you."

"Why don't you go with him? Get some fresh air, dear?"

"I'd rather just have a lie-down, thank you, Mother. Don't worry. I'll come downstairs for elevenses."

It seemed like her mother was moving at half speed

as she smiled, leaned forwards, kissed her on the forehead, glanced around the bedroom in her usual way and then turned to leave. Charlotte forced herself to wait until she'd counted to two before shutting the door carefully and quietly, lest she seem too eager to shut her mother out. She'd only get suspicious.

By the time Charlotte was back into position and looking down into the room, Ben had only managed to make the wick smoulder slightly. "I think I'm rather nervous," he said to Master Judicant, who just nodded.

Charlotte drew the air deep into her lungs, released it, knew she could do this. All she had to do was focus on the wick and—

The flame burst into existence at the tip of the wick with such violence that Master Judicant jolted to his feet. Charlotte could feel the rush of heat through the small gaps in the plaster and struggled to contain what she'd created. Ben, to his credit, kept his eyes focused firmly on the candle, but his knuckles turned white as he gripped the edge of the table. Master Judicant muttered something about fetching the magus and then Charlotte managed to withdraw her power, leaving naught but a normal flame, wavering a little. By the time she felt fully detached from it, half the candle had burned down and a pool of wax was solidifying around it.

Mother's table! Charlotte bit her lip, feeling guilty, as

Master Judicant went to the door and called Ainsworth back in.

"A resounding success!" he cheered and the magus hurried back in from where she'd been standing in the hallway.

"Good grief!" She gasped at the sight of the candle. "A most impressive demonstration, young man! Most impressive indeed!"

"I'm sorry it took a little while," Ben said. "Nerves, I think."

The magus smiled, snuffing out the flame with a mere glance. "Never you mind, young man, you got there in the end. Are you satisfied all was in order, Master Judicant?"

"I am. Well done," he said to Ben with a broad smile. "Only one in ten show that sort of ability, and you managed to keep control. An excellent start."

"It's clear you have a place in our discipline, should you accept our offer," Ainsworth said. "And tell your parents we'll get the table French polished as an apology."

Ben laughed and Charlotte smiled at the sound of it. He was standing straighter; even the slight stoop he'd adopted in his youth to hide the fact that he was so much taller than everyone else had gone. For the first time, Charlotte genuinely felt hope for her brother's future.

Chapter 11

ONCE MAGUS ANSWORTH HAD left, the family and Master Judicant enjoyed elevenses together. There was laughter and chatter and Charlotte noted the way Master Judicant smiled more at Ben. He was impressed, genuinely so. And Ben didn't seem too tired at all. For a little while, Charlotte forgot about the cell and the conspiracy, the threat to her father and the magnitude of the crime she was committing in tricking the magi. It was blissful.

As Charlotte cleared away the tea things, the knock on the door brought her heart back to earth. Her father greeted Magus Hopkins, and she made sure she was in the kitchen when he was invited in. She didn't want to be distracted by him. It was time to focus once more.

Making the same excuse as before would be suspicious, so she waited as long as she could, giving the magus time to settle and arrange his test.

"I'm going to take a stroll," she said to her parents. "Would either of you like to join me?"

"I'm finishing a bodice in the living room," Mother said. "And I'd like Father to stay at home whilst the tests are being done. But you go out, dear."

"I'll just walk a couple of streets down and back," Charlotte said. "I just need some fresh air. Oh. I left my shawl upstairs."

It was a flimsy excuse, but enough to get her back in her room and spying through the ceiling rose once more.

"You've seen another example of one of these before," Magus Hopkins was saying as he placed a timepiece on the table. It was a clock, the sort that only the very wealthiest had in their homes. Not only was the clock itself expensive, but so was the stipend paid to the local magus to keep it running to time. It was made from mahogany, curved in an elegant arch shape around the face of the clock and sloping down to a solid rectangular base. From her vantage point, Charlotte couldn't see anything of the decoration on the front. "It works on a similar principle to the timepiece you altered accidentally. I'm going to remove the cover at the back to expose the workings and your task is to identify and move the correct parts of the mechanism to change the time displayed. I fully expect you to fail."

"Magus Hopkins." Master Judicant's voice was low and stern. "You must not make any further comments about your expectations of success or failure."

"Apologies, sir." Hopkins looked up at the ceiling, as if trying to think of another way to put what he planned to say, and Charlotte drew back fearfully, convinced he could see her through the gaps. "The temptation is to adjust the hands on the clock directly. I caution you against that as they are very fragile and break easily. The mechanism inside is more robust and able to cope with . . . untrained attempts. I urge you to focus your efforts there."

He twisted the clock around and opened the small door at the back with a tiny key. "I don't usually give this as a test to Latents, but as you have already shown an admirable affinity to this sort of mechanism, I felt it was appropriate."

Charlotte bit her lip in frustration. Even with the opera glasses, she couldn't look through the wood and see inside the clock.

"If I fail this, will I be permitted to try the usual test?"

"With Master Judicant's permission, yes. Timekeepers are in great demand, Mr Gunn. Should you prove to be talented in this area, my college will permit me to make a higher offer of compensation to your family. If you don't wish to try this, you may of course refuse and I'll give you something far less impressive to achieve."

Charlotte looked at Master Judicant. He didn't look entirely happy. It seemed that Hopkins was pushing boundaries but not so far that he could be pushed back. "How do you wish to proceed, Latent?" he asked, and Charlotte liked him that little bit more. He was willing to give Ben the choice.

"I'll try it," Ben said, and Charlotte's heart sank. How could she help him without seeing the mechanism?

"Splendid." Magus Hopkins stood. "I will leave you to your efforts. It's less dangerous than a test of Thermaturgy or Dynamics, so I may go for a brief stroll, if that's acceptable, Master Judicant?"

Master Judicant nodded his assent and Hopkins left. Master Judicant moved the clock to a different position on the table and Ben sat in place, staring inside.

Charlotte opened the wooden chest behind her and rifled through the contents until she found the right sketchbook. It was a desperate plan, but she hoped that if she could see the mechanism she'd drawn from the timepiece, she might be able to try something with the clock below.

There was a knock on the front door as she flipped through the pages, looking for the best sketch. It was loud and frantic, making her pause. Surely the debt collector wasn't going to come early?

"Mrs Gunn!" It was Billy, who lived next door. The boy's voice could be heard through the glass of her bedroom window that overlooked the street. "Mr Gunn!" He hammered again.

The door was opened and Charlotte could hear the soft tones of Hopkins's voice but not well enough to understand what he was saying.

"Me gran!" the boy said on the doorstep. He was crying. "She's dead! I dunno what to do! Please help!"

Charlotte abandoned the sketchbook, put the floorboard back into place silently and covered it with the rug as the sound of her parents comforting the boy came from downstairs. She hurried down, past Hopkins, who had drawn back to the foot of the stairs to remove himself from the drama.

Billy was sobbing on the doorstep. Mother wrapped her arms around him as Father put on his boots. "She was ill, but not that bad. Then this mornin' she couldn't get out of bed and then I made her a cuppa and took it up and she told me to go and do me round and she'd be fine. I just got back and she's all . . . she's . . ." He broke down and sobbed into Mother's shoulder.

"I'll take care of everything," Father said.

The door to the dining room opened and Ben came out, ignoring Master Judicant's protestations. "What's happened? Who's died?"

"Mrs Cartwright," Charlotte said, going to his side.

"Come into the kitchen and have a cup of tea," Mother said to Billy. "I've got a spare currant bun in the tin. Come and warm yourself up by the stove. Mr Gunn will send for the right people."

Ben put an arm round Charlotte's shoulder as they watched the boy being steered through the house. Billy's parents died shortly after Ben had returned home, struck by the same flu that had ravaged the neighbourhood early that year. What would happen to him now? Poor child.

"I'm sorry, Master Judicant," Ben said, turning to speak to him as he came to the doorway. "It's our next-door neighbour. She died. Could I have a moment?"

Master Judicant nodded. "Come back inside when you're ready."

Charlotte watched him go back in to take his place and realised that the mechanism was in plain sight, only a couple of yards away. She drank in as many details as she could in as long a glance as she dared risk, and then shut the dining room door.

"I'm not sure I can do this one, Charlie," Ben whispered to her as he embraced her.

"Try your best," she whispered back. "It's all going to be fine."

He went back into the dining room and Charlotte looked over to Magus Hopkins, but he wasn't by the stairs. The front door was still open, so she guessed he'd gone out for the walk. She closed it, checked on Billy, who was being cared for in the kitchen and then went back to the hall, planning to sneak upstairs to work on the clock. To her surprise, Magus Hopkins was standing at the bottom of the stairs again, doing up the buttons of his burgundy coat.

"Oh, I thought you'd gone out, Magus Hopkins."

"I'm just about to." He smiled, a brief smile that had a hint of self-satisfaction, and then left.

Altering the clock's mechanism from memory, rather than sight, was the hardest task she'd ever attempted. She stared down at the top of the clock, trying to imagine what the mechanism inside would look like from above. She wasn't even entirely sure which parts made the hands turn—she hadn't intended to make the first timepiece change, after all—so all she could do was try to deduce which parts looked like they could move. In the end, she settled upon two small cogs that clearly interacted with each other in the timepiece she'd sketched and looked similar to what she'd seen briefly downstairs. After a couple of minutes that didn't seem to be making anything except a headache happen, she saw Master Judicant lean forwards, checking the hands of the clock. There was the hint of a smile, so she forced her concentration to its sharpest peak and was rewarded with a horrible grinding sound from the clock.

"I think it best to stop there, Latent," Master Judicant said. "You've moved the hands enough to pass the test."

Hopkins was summoned back into the room once he'd returned from his walk and, with raised eyebrows, noted the time the hands displayed. "Well," he said, surprised. "A remarkable feat." He turned it and peered inside to look at the mechanism. Charlotte mirrored his wince. "And that's why we don't usually do this sort of test," he muttered. "Jolly good, Latent. I will report back to my college and an offer will be with you in the morning."

"Thank you," Ben said, doing his best to seem responsible and slightly guilty about the broken clock.

It was only when Hopkins left that Charlotte realised how much the test had tired her out. She took off the crinoline cage, lay on the bed and dozed off, worrying about Billy and where he would go, wondering what Magus Ledbetter's test would be and making rudimentary plans to sneak back to the cell in the small hours and alter the mechanism.

The sound of the front door slamming shut woke her with a start. Magus Ledbetter's booming voice rumbled through the house and Charlotte sat up, suddenly alert. The quilted coverlet that her grandmother had sewn was covering her, and she realised that her mother must have found her fast asleep and covered her up. Thank goodness she'd had the presence of mind to replace the floorboard and rug before she'd let herself rest.

Magus Ledbetter didn't waste any time on pleasantries, and the door to the dining room was shut before Charlotte had folded away the coverlet. Soon she was back in spying position, though she didn't have to listen as carefully to hear his instructions.

"As I told you yesterday, son, the esoteric art of Dynamics is all about strength, coordination and concentration. Not physical strength, mind you, but mental strength. Now, being an untrained Latent makes it far more likely that a test of ability for this college is dangerous, so we like to ask candidates to do something small. Not the sort of thing them Kinetics fuss with, something that can't do much damage is all."

He, too, had a leather case—his was brown with a rectangular shape embossed below the clasp and outlined in red. Charlotte grabbed her opera glasses, but by the time she'd returned to spy through them, the case had been laid flat. Ledbetter took out a long wooden box and slid off the lid, which again had something embossed onto it. He removed a curved wedge of wood that looked like one of half of the letter C, with two grooves carved into it. Then he took out two perfectly spherical metal balls the size of walnuts and dropped them into place at the bottom of both grooves, making a heavy *thunk* sound.

"It's simple enough," Ledbetter continued. "All you have to do is push these balls up the curve of the wood. Start with just the one, I'd say, and if you're able, move the two of them. If you can push one of them up, don't worry about keeping it there. It's all about you having the mental strength to fight gravity. Understand?"

Ben nodded and Magus Ledbetter looked to Master

Judicant for confirmation he'd explained everything to his satisfaction. At Master Judicant's nod, Ledbetter excused himself and went out of the room. As with all the other tests, Master Judicant moved the materials into a different position on the table—presumably to stop the Magus influencing anything with the memory of its location—and gave Ben the nod to start.

Charlotte started to focus and then was distracted by the sound of Magus Ledbetter stomping through the house to the kitchen, probably in search of a slice of cake. As she attempted to gather her thoughts again, Charlotte's gaze brushed across the lid of the box that had been left next to the case. Curious, she peered at the rectangular shape through the opera glasses.

It was the same design as the hallmark she had seen embossed into the lid and base of the debt collector's cell, and the sight of it made her freeze. For a moment, she doubted herself. Surely it was a mistake? But no, she had drawn that exact pattern of overlapping symbols, the marks of her pencil on the paper of her notebook clarifying the blurred shapes in the metal into the very same design she was looking at now.

Magus Ledbetter was involved? Then she remembered the name of the doctor who had signed off all the deaths at that house, how she'd thought it mere coincidence, given the common name, but now it seemed to be far more than that. Brothers, perhaps? Cousins? Was the conspiracy of murder being kept within the family as far as possible? Whatever the arrangement, it was clear that the magus and the doctor were colluding to hide the deaths of those poor people from the authorities. What an abuse of power and privilege!

The rage she'd felt the night before as she'd listened to those foul men discussing the monetary benefits of murder began to rise again. She remembered the young magus talking about his "guvnor" and how he'd described him as a "bullying old bastard," and then any ordered thoughts were buried beneath a fury that had remained unexpressed for far too long.

The metal balls rattled in the grooves and then shot up the curved wood so fast she lost sight of them before hearing a smash of glass. She only connected the two a beat later. Master Judicant yelled out, calling to Ben to stop, as the lid displaying the hallmark cracked in two, rapidly followed by the dining room table. The case, the smashed box, the curved wooden slope, all came crashing down as the two halves of the table collapsed inwards.

"Magus Ledbetter!" Master Judicant called, rushing to the door. "Magus Ledbetter! We need your assistance!"

Ben had stood up now and was shouting, too. "I'm sorry! I'm sorry! I want it to stop!"

His distress penetrated enough to make her try to rein

herself in, but it was so hard. Charlotte looked away from the room below, focusing instead on the wooden chest in her room and squealed when a crack splintered through its lid. She squeezed her eyes shut, clenching her fists, imagining herself folding inwards, shrinking back inside herself, until she was left with a pain in her chest and a better sense of control.

"Blood and sand!" Ledbetter boomed from the doorway into the dining room as he took in the wreckage. "You put the balls through the bloody window!"

"I'm sorry," Ben stammered. "I didn't mean to—"

"Don't be sorry, ye silly beggar! That was bloody marvellous! Well done, lad!" Ledbetter gripped Ben's hand and pumped it up and down, the handshake nearly knocking Ben over. "Never in all my days have I seen a test passed so bloody well! And don't worry about all this." He waved a hand at the table. "It's just 'cos your untrained. We'll give you a mark and it'll help keep you focused. Don't be afraid of your power, son. D'ye hear?"

The sight of him still shaking Ben's hand made Charlotte feel sick. That rectangular shape, was that Ledbetter's "mark"? Or did it mean the entire college of Dynamics? She'd leapt to the conclusion that Ledbetter was personally involved and she shouldn't have. All that damage, just because she'd leapt to a conclusion without checking first.

Her head pounded and she couldn't stop shaking. Charlotte pulled away from the gap in the floorboards to lie next to it as the room started to spin. Ledbetter's voice rose up through the gaps, denying her rest.

"You're on the brink of turning wild, boy. Your father did the right thing. Now you can see why this is so important. Don't try anything else now, not a thing, you hear me? It's not safe. Now, rest up, you look like you're about to keel over. I'll be in touch with the offer from my college. I'll see you tomorrow! Good day to you, Master Judicant."

The front door slammed shut moments later and she listened to the magus whistling merrily as he strode off down the street. There was the sound of her mother fussing over Ben downstairs, Father and Master Judicant talking about the broken window and the table, and it all felt too loud, too much. Charlotte pressed her temples with her fists and started to cry. What if it wasn't all lies, like the man at Speaker's Corner said? What if she was turning wild?

Chapter 12

CHARLOTTE HELD UP THE candle to the mechanism, still panting from the exertion of lifting it out of the space below the cell and clicking it into place so it didn't retract once more. It was long past midnight and she was shaking with fear, but she had to do this. She couldn't let her father die.

Examining the central dial and comparing it to the sketch, she noticed that Magus Hopkins hadn't just added a couple of arrows to mark where she needed to change the mechanism; he'd added details to the markings on the dial itself.

It wasn't difficult to make the adjustments; in fact, it seemed to have been designed to have a variety of settings. That Hopkins knew what the markings on the dial were worried her, until she realised that it may simply be a common part used in several different machines, just as she'd seen in the timepieces. Ben had mentioned to her that trains and factory machinery contained the same parts, simply arranged differently to suit their purpose. She wished she understood what this machine did, but it wasn't the time to lament her ignorance. At least if the worst happened and she couldn't persuade her parents to visit their family in the southwest once Ben had made his choice, her father wouldn't die. At worst, he would be put in debtor's prison once he'd seen the magistrate, and then the money from Ben's recruitment would come through and the debt would be paid. All that would be left to fathom was a way to put an end to the conspiracy. Perhaps an anonymous letter to Master Judicant would suffice, a few days after Ben's recruitment. At least there was hope again.

Once she was done, Charlotte lowered the mechanism back into place and screwed the plate back into position, using a screwdriver she'd borrowed from her father's dusty tool box. She didn't dare risk using any esoteric arts, not after what Ledbetter had said.

After packing away the sketchbook in her satchel and closing the unlocked cell door so all was as she had found it, Charlotte went to the window, blew the candle out and opened the curtains. As she climbed out, the satchel strap got caught on the clasp and in frustration, she wriggled herself free of the bag and tossed it out into the yard ahead of her.

Just as she was climbing out, the fabric of her dress got caught on the same clasp. With one leg inside and one leg dangling out of the window, it was the worst possible time. Cursing women's clothing everywhere beneath her breath, Charlotte struggled to twist around and untangle it, just as the sound of one of the front door locks being tumbled echoed through the house.

Panicking, she tried to find where her dress hem was snagged, but there was so much fabric it was impossible. She heard the front door creak—had all the other locks been left open?—and desperately tugged at the dress. She heard it tear but not enough, banged her head on the lower sash of the window and gave the dress another yank, making another impressive tearing sound as the young magus and his father came into the room.

"It's a bleedin' girl!" said the magus, just as Charlotte managed to rip the last of the dress free.

The window sash slammed down on her leg with a wave of the magus's hand, and she cried out. The father grabbed her booted foot, the window sash was moved up again and she was pulled back into the room and thrown onto the floorboards. Her leg throbbed, as did her head, and when she tried to get to her feet, the magus pushed her over again with a rough shove to her shoulder.

"Bloody hell! It's that bloke's daughter!" said the broom-moustached man, holding the lantern up to her face. "What you doin' 'ere?"

"I . . . I came to ask that you give my father more time to pay the debt!"

"At half one in the bleedin' mornin'?" The man laughed mirthlessly. "You gotta come up with summat better than that!"

The magus looked at the cell and back at her. "Was it you who broke in yesterday?"

"I beg your pardon?"

"We was tipped off," the father said. "Who sent you?"

"No one sent me! I told you, I want you to give my father more time to pay his debt!"

"Who's her father?" the magus asked.

"Mr Gunn, the one we talked about."

The magus knew her name—Charlotte could see the flash of recognition on his face. "Was it Hopkins that sent you?" the magus said, grabbing her coat at the collar and hauling her to her feet. He was much stronger than he looked.

"No! He doesn't know anything about the debt! I found the address on the letter you gave me!" she said to his father. The magus hadn't let go and his grip had tightened the collar uncomfortably. "Please, I just couldn't sleep and I thought I could find out how much he owed and leave you a letter . . ." It sounded terrible, even as she said it, but she simply couldn't think quickly enough.

"This is all bollocks," the father said. "Who's this Hopkins?"

"Another magus, a dodgy one," his son replied. "He

don't like my guvnor and the feelin' is mutual. I reckon he's got her to come 'ere and snoop about."

The father tugged at his moustache. "Don't like this. What kind of scum sends a girl to do his dirty work?"

"What did he tell you to do?" the magus yelled at her, shaking her until her collar started to choke her. She clawed at his hands, coughing.

"Nothing," she gasped. "Let me go!"

The magus dragged her across the room, opened the cell door and threw her inside, slamming her against the bars so hard it knocked the wind out of her.

"Son? What you doin'?"

"My guvnor said no one could find out what was goin' on 'ere. No one. This stinks of Hopkins. I've heard about this Gunn family, about her brother bein' tested and turnin' out to be some bloomin' prodigy or summat, and Hopkins was one of the testers. I reckon she blabbed to 'im about Daddy's debt, flutterin' her eyelashes, beggin' 'im for help, and he said he would if she came 'ere an' sniffed about." He closed the cell door and held it shut. "What did you find last night? Were you 'ere the same time as us?"

Charlotte just rubbed the back of her head and tried to look too dazed to reply as she struggled to think of what to do. Should she make the lantern explode? No, she might burn that man, and odious as he was, she'd never be able to live with herself if she did.

The son fished the keys from his pocket.

"Son? Are you sure this is a good idea?"

"I can't take the risk. The guvnor will kill me if she blabs to anyone."

"She might 'ave already!" the father said.

"Then this is 'er comeuppance." The magus sneered.

"But she'll die!" the father said, putting a hand on his shoulder. "I 'ent ever locked a lady in this cell. It don't feel right, son. She 'ent done nothin' wrong! It was her dad who—"

"Shut up," the magus said to his father, and pushed a key into the lock.

Charlotte scrabbled to her feet, praying that she had remembered Magus Hopkins's words correctly and that his suggested changes had actually disabled the device. "Please, I just want to go home!" she said to the father. Even though the cage hopefully wasn't going to kill her now, she had no desire to spend a night in it, not at the mercy of this cruel magus.

"Son," the man said, putting a hand on the magus's shoulder as he turned the key in the lock.

It clicked, loudly, and through the metal beneath her, Charlotte could feel the mechanism clunking away, activated somehow by the locking of the cell. The magus grinned through the bars at her. "This'll teach ya for working with that bastard Hopkins. Feel that? It'll get worse. Soon you'll feel like water goin' down a plughole. And then . . ."

He stopped, his face draining of colour so rapidly it was frightening to watch. His father set the lantern down, grabbing one of the bars to steady himself, as the florid broken veins across his nose started to fade.

"I don't under—" The magus croaked and then collapsed, falling against his father as he fell, too.

Charlotte watched their eyes, the brief panic and then the sudden, subtle shift as the life left their bodies. She clamped a hand over her mouth to trap the scream, realising what had happened as the clunking sounds of the mechanism below came to a stop. Hopkins had lied to her. She hadn't rendered the mechanism harmless—she had just pushed the lethal effect outside the cage. She stared at the two dead bodies, noticed how a spider next to the lantern had also curled up, dead, and burst into tears.

Chapter 13

CHARLOTTE DIDN'T SLEEP THAT night, and feared that she would never sleep again. She'd sat in the cage until the tears and the shaking had stopped, then plucked the keys from the dead magus's pocket and unlocked the cage door. It took some time for her to muster the courage to step outside of it, she was so fearful the effect would still be active. It seemed it was all over, though; the mechanism was silent once more and she suffered no ill effects when she left the cell.

She had wanted to flee as swiftly as she could, not just from that awful house, but London, too. She couldn't abandon her family, though, nor George, and where would she go? Once the panic subsided, she decided that no one knew she was here or what had happened, and if Hopkins suspected her, there was no proof. Besides, she'd done what he suggested; he was hardly going to march her to the Peelers.

Then a strange calm descended over her and she went to the filing cabinet in the front office, using the debt collector's lantern to guide her way. She found a file of "open debts" which included details of her father's loan and five others. With the owner of the business dead, surely the other sons he mentioned would be tasked with going through his affairs? If they found this file, the threat to her father wouldn't be ended, and she couldn't bear the thought of the people in the file being put at the same risk as her father.

She flipped through the other folders in the cabinet, saw that the ones who'd paid had the word stamped at the top of the page. She found ink and the appropriate stamper in the desk and then she knew what to do.

Now she was lying in her bed, still shivering periodically, that file of "open debts" empty and the former contents all stamped with "PAID" across the top and filed appropriately. She knew enough to fear that once ledgers and accounts had been pored over, the discrepancies would be noticed, but perhaps it would be too late by then.

So she was a forger and a murderer now. Even though she'd made sure that all traces of her presence had been removed from the house—even down to the scrap of her skirt hem trapped in the window clasp—surely it was just a matter of time before the Peelers came for her. And if not them, the Enforcers. She knuckled her gritty eyes, unable to weep any more. She could only hope that she'd done enough to save her family before whatever punishment was meted out for her.

It was still dark when she heard Ben moving around in his bedroom. The poor lamb probably couldn't sleep, either. When she heard him go downstairs, she dressed and followed him down.

She found him sitting in the dining room, the gas lamps newly lit. The broken dining table had been cleared to the side of the room and propped up against the wall until Father decided what to do with it. Ledbetter's case and the cracked wooden box rested next to it. Ben was sitting in one of the chairs, elbows on knees, staring at the lid of the wooden box. Just the sight of the rectangular mark on it made Charlotte feel sick.

"Can't sleep, dear heart?" he said, twisting to smile at her. His eyes widened and she realised she must look terrible. "Have you been crying?"

Charlotte nodded. She opened her mouth to confess it all, but then stopped herself. He didn't need this burden. He had to focus on his own future. And besides, there was nothing to be done about it now. "Everything is going to change," she finally said. It was truthful, at least.

"For the better, Charlie." Ben smiled. "I think the offers are going to be high." He lowered his voice. "You did such a splendid job. Perhaps a little too splendid towards the end." He looked at the lid of the box again. "Magus Ledbetter seemed pleased, though, even though his box got broken."

"Is that the mark of the Dynamics college?"

He shook his head. "No, it's his personal mark. He told me a little about them in my interview. Desperately interesting stuff. It's all to do with focus."

"Could someone else put his mark on something and then . . . make it work without him knowing it?"

"I asked the very same question." Ben grinned. "I couldn't understand why he would have such a personal symbol in plain sight. He told me that anyone can look at it, but only he knows what all the different symbols mean. It's also called a . . . sigil, I think he said. Knowing what the different parts are, why they overlap, why they are in the mark in the first place, that's what focuses the power."

Charlotte swallowed. "So another could put that mark on something, but it wouldn't work unless they know what it means?"

Ben smiled. "I think so. Magus Ledbetter gave me the impression that it's far more complicated than that, but I think that's the essence of it."

"I don't think you should go into the college of Dynamics."

"Why ever not?"

Charlotte looked at the mark on the broken lid. "I don't trust Magus Ledbetter."

Ben looked distinctly unimpressed. "You've barely

spoken to him. You never liked loud men. Mother said they used to make you cry when you were a baby."

"It's nothing like that!"

The clock towers chimed six o'clock and Ben stretched. "We will all sleep better tonight, I wager."

"I mean it, Ben, I don't think you—"

There was the sound of letters being posted through the door and Ben shot out of the room faster than she'd ever seen him move. Charlotte went to the window and saw a courier from the Royal Society of Esoteric Arts jogging away.

To her surprise, Ben took the letters straight up to his room and closed the door. She folded her arms, frustrated, and then went to make some tea. She could hear her parents starting to move about; soon everyone would want breakfast. She might as well make herself useful.

A short time later, she and her parents were squashed around the kitchen table with bread and butter, bacon and poached eggs, none of which Charlotte could stomach. There was no conversation, all of them wondering what the offers would be and how their lives would be changed. Just as Father started to tackle the bacon, Ben came to the doorway.

"I've made my decision."

"Aren't you going to discuss it with us first?" Charlotte asked, irritated.

"Now, now, Charlie," Father said, patting her hand. "It's his choice to make."

"It wasn't as difficult as I thought it would be," Ben said, pulling up the last stool and perching on it between Mother and Father. He held the three letters in his hand, pulled one out and rested it on the table. "Magus Hopkins, from the College of Fine Kinetics, offers one hundred and fifty pounds to the family upon my acceptance."

Mother gasped as Father grinned. "Go on, son," he said.

"He wrote a very nice letter," Ben continued. "He said he was very surprised by how gifted I actually was and that I would be a fine addition to the Royal Society. He didn't mention the broken clock at all."

Charlotte buttered a slice of bread so vigorously in her anger that the knife tore a hole in the centre of it. "I still don't trust him," she muttered, but no one seemed to hear.

Ben put the second letter on the table. "Magus Ainsworth says that the College of Thermaturgy is willing to compensate the family with three hundred pounds upon my acceptance."

"Pour me a cup of tea, Charlie," Mother said in a wavering voice. "Three hundred pounds?"

Ben nodded, smiling. "She says in the letter that she's

never seen such a talented Latent and that I'll have a fine future in the Royal Society."

Charlotte watched him beam at their parents, as if the praise had genuinely been meant for him. Had he forgotten that it was her power that had impressed the magi? She pressed her lips together, unable to correct him in front of their parents.

"And lastly," Ben said, laying down the third envelope, "Magus Ledbetter has offered our family one thousand pounds to compensate for my immediate acceptance into the College of Dynamics."

Mother's teacup slipped from her hand and smashed on the tiled floor. Father's mouth hung open, slack, as Ben grinned.

"We could rent a furnished house in the West End," Mother said, her voice high with excitement. "And your trousseau and wedding would be the best the family has ever seen!" she said to Charlotte. "You could marry right away! We could pay a deposit on a fine house for you and George and help with the rent until he's promoted!"

"You could give up the sewing," Father said to Mother, and she started to weep.

"You haven't chosen Ledbetter, have you?" Charlotte asked.

"Of course I have! He said that he can make me one of the finest practitioners of Dynamics the Empire has ever seen. And the Dynamics magi are the most successful in-dustrialists. He says in the letter he'll tutor me personally, and show me how to design and run my own mill. I can combine it with engineering! It's perfect!"

"But . . . but I don't think he's a good man, Ben," Char-lotte said as her parents embraced each other and started laughing and weeping together.

"You've made a rash judgement," Ben said, cross with her reaction. "This is the best thing for our family."

"Are you sure it's a thousand?" Father said suddenly. "It must be a mistake! That's a fortune!"

"He's one of the wealthiest men in Britain," Ben said. "Look at the letter. The offer is from the College, but he's personally increased it with his own private money, he's so keen for me to join."

"Or to keep you out of the other colleges," Charlotte said, thinking of the way the magus had spoken of Hop-kins the night before.

"What does it matter?" Ben said. "I'm accepting it. I've already penned the letter and the courier will be here very soon to collect it."

Charlotte slammed her butter knife down on the table. "May I speak with you in private?" she said to Ben, and went out into the hallway.

After a brief exchange with their parents, Ben followed her out to the bottom of the stairs. "Why are you so sour,

Charlie? This is exactly what you wanted!"

"You were speaking as if they chose you for something you had done!"

He frowned. "How else am I to behave?"

"But it's not real! You can't possibly accept a thousand pounds under false pretences!"

He paused, looking down at his feet. "You yourself told me that they expect a drop in ability. How can you be so fickle? We work so hard for this and when it's a resounding success, you're upset? It makes no sense!" When she said nothing, he added, "Besides, doesn't what happened yesterday make you question your decision to keep hidden? You heard what Magus Ledbetter said about turning wild. Is that why you're so against him?"

"No, it is not," Charlotte said, wishing she could explain the real reason for her distrust of Ledbetter, and Hopkins, too. "I think you should accept Magus Ainsworth's offer. Thermaturgy is where your genuine talent lies."

"No. It's Dynamics for me, Charlie. I'll work at it, I will, and I'll become one of the great industrialists, too." He held her shoulders. "Let me be a success, just for once, please? Didn't you see the way Mother and Father looked at me? Like I was finally something to be proud of? And this fortune will change their lives, and yours!"

"I was always proud of you."

His face softened and he pulled her into a fierce embrace. "I won't let you down, Charlie Bean. You gave me this chance and I'm going to take it. I'll be the magus Ledbetter thinks I can be and the brother you deserve and a son to be proud of."

Charlotte held him tight, knowing she wasn't going to dissuade him, no matter what she said. "I love you," she whispered.

"I love you, too."

There was a knock at the door and Ben released her to answer it. The courier Charlotte had seen earlier stood to attention. "Do you have a reply for the Royal Society, sir?"

Ben reached into his jacket pocket and pulled out the letter. "I'll pack right away," he added and the courier nodded.

"There will be a carriage to collect you within the hour, sir. Good day to you. And congratulations!"

Chapter 14

CHARLOTTE HAD DONE HER best to comfort her mother, who hadn't stopped crying since they'd waved Ben off, but there was nothing more to do or say. He was gone and all they could do was hope that he thrived there. After managing only half a cup of tea, Charlotte decided she had to get out of the house. She was exhausted but too distressed to rest. A long walk was the only thing she could face.

Her father came to her as she put on her coat. "Going to tell George the good news?"

"After a long walk," she said, trying to hide how she felt.

"I think my letter worked," he whispered to her, after checking Mother wasn't nearby. "The debt collector didn't come, and he was always very punctual."

Charlotte weathered another wave of nausea. "Hopefully it will all be resolved amicably," she said carefully. "I'll see you later, Papa."

"Charlie." He caught her arm gently as she went to the door. "Thank you for being so good about the debt.

I haven't been able to give you everything I wanted to when you were growing up. That's going to change now."

She smiled sadly. "I don't need anything, Papa. I just want you to be happy and safe." She kissed him on the cheek and went out.

Charlotte didn't have a destination in mind; she just needed to move. It was a brilliantly bright winter's day, the sky blue and the wind cold. Without even thinking about it, she found herself in the same street as the bakery and bookshop. She took a breath to suggest to Ben that they get a currant bun and then remembered he wasn't with her.

The bakery was closed "indefinitely" according to a notice on the door. A woman passing by said, "You'd better find another bakery, love. The baker topped 'erself."

"I beg your pardon?"

"Her boy was one of them magi. They tested him and he was and she was called to trial. They found her hanging in the back room before they could get her in the dock. Terrible business."

The woman left her reeling. Charlotte looked inside; the dustpan of glass she'd swept up herself was where she'd left it, as was the chair where she'd sat the baker down. Would that woman have held on if Charlotte had come back to visit, as she'd promised? She covered her mouth, trying not to cry. No, she was just a stranger to that poor woman. How vain of her to think a visit could have made a difference.

She drifted across the street. *Love, Death and Other Magicks* was still being displayed in the bookshop window. She stared at the pictures, trying to match the person she had been when she drew them to the person she was now. Artist to criminal in just a few short weeks.

"They're beautiful illustrations."

The voice of Magus Hopkins made her yelp in surprise. She stepped away from him, keeping her back to him.

"That Charles Baker chap is very talented, isn't he?" he pressed but she remained silent. "Such a keen eye for detail. And the expressions on the faces are exquisite. I've never seen—"

"I do not wish to speak to you, sir," Charlotte said, walking away. She had to keep her anger in check.

"But I wish to speak to you," the magus said, falling into step alongside her. "It's most important that I do."

The pavement was crowded with people, and she noticed how many of them were staring at him in his fine clothes. "My brother has made his choice and there is nothing to be discussed." She didn't want to talk about the machine or what had happened at number six, New Road, not here, not now.

"But I have something to return to you." He produced

a horribly familiar sketchbook from behind his back, making her stop. It was the one usually hidden at the bottom of the wooden chest in her room. "You have a very distinctive style, Miss Gunn. Such a keen eye for detail. And the sketches of the timepiece in particular are most impressive."

She couldn't stop the fearsome blush from spreading across her cheeks. "How did you get that?"

"I stole it from your room. How else would I come by it?"

For a moment, all she could do was blink at his audacity. "You are one of the very worst examples of a man given too much privilege," she finally said.

"You are one of the most dangerous young women in this city," he replied calmly. "Now, may I suggest we continue this exchange of insults in the carriage over there, rather than on the street? I have a suspicion that you actually have a great deal to say to me, and privacy will be preferable."

She folded her arms. "If you think I am going to get into a carriage alone with you, then you are, quite frankly, an idiot."

He smiled. How could God have made such an odious man so beautiful? "If you think I am going to let you walk away without having this conversation with me, you are, too, Miss Gunn. Come now." He held out his hand. "We can be perfectly civil to each other, surely?"

Perhaps he was the devil. Either way, it was clear he knew what she had done, now that he'd seen her sketches of the timepiece. And perhaps giving him her honest opinion of him would be quite a relief. She sighed, resigned, and marched towards the waiting carriage.

It was an impressive Clarence carriage, large enough to carry four people but empty inside. In contrast to the black exterior, the seats inside were a beautiful royal blue and the doors were inlaid with walnut. The driver was dressed in black and showed no interest in who the magus was inviting into his carriage. The four horses that pulled it were fine specimens, all dark brown and shining with health. She wondered why Hopkins wasn't using esoteric means to travel about London, but then perhaps that would make it harder to do what he was doing without drawing attention.

As Charlotte climbed inside, she wondered if this was the last time she'd be seen alive on a London street. She paused, considering whether to just open the opposite door and climb straight out, but then Hopkins was seating himself down, having closed the door behind him. She took a step towards the other door just as he knocked on the roof and the carriage pulled away. She plopped into the seat across from him inelegantly, making him smile. She scowled back.

"So, you're a Latent," he said casually, as if it were the most humdrum thing in the world. "One who has just successfully conned the Royal Society into paying an extraordinary amount for a very average young man." He stared at her as she sank into the seat. Then he started to clap. "Bravo, Miss Gunn, bravo."

Confused, she kept her mouth shut, convinced that anything she said in response would damn her.

"How did it go at the house in New Road last night?"

The decision to stay quiet was instantly forgotten. "You are the most despicable man I have ever had the misfortune to meet! You said it would be rendered harmless!"

"Ah, so you changed the settings on the device?"

She took a breath to answer, but paused. It felt as if he were a cat poised to pounce, watching with amusement as she scurried back and forth like a mouse trapped between his paws. He was leaping from one topic to another, as if batting her with a paw to see which way she ran, just for his entertainment.

"You disgusting man," she said, tears welling. "You think this is amusing? To trick a woman into killing because you were too cowardly to act? To damn her soul in the process? I'm bound for the fires of hell because—"

"Oh, don't be so ridiculous." He sighed. "All of that eternal damnation nonsense is really too tiresome for words. You acted innocently, if that is of such concern to you, and rid the world of two creatures who have inflicted far more suffering than I ever have."

"You lied to me!"

"I did nothing of the sort. The changes to the settings did render it harmless. For anyone inside the cage."

"I could have been killed!"

"I had no idea you would be put inside it by the very men I sought to outsmart! I was merely concerned with keeping your father alive—he was the next one destined to be its prisoner, not you!"

She sat back, considering what he'd said. How could he have known they would be there that night? Perhaps it wasn't him using her to strike a blow against his enemies, as she'd thought. "Did you know Ledbetter is involved?"

"I suspected as much, given his mark was in your other sketchbook."

"Then why didn't you warn me?"

"To what end? What would you have done when he visited the house the next day to test your brother? Challenged him? Set fire to him?"

"I . . ."

"My dear Miss Gunn, there are times for open accusations, and this was definitely not one of them."

"But my brother has chosen Ledbetter's offer!"

"Of course he has," Hopkins said, tugging at the fingers of a glove to take it off. "Ledbetter didn't want me to gain such a talented apprentice, so he made an offer your brother couldn't possibly refuse. But that's not what I wanted to talk to you about."

"Wait. I killed two men because of you and that's all you have to say about it? Won't Ledbetter find out what I did? One of them was his apprentice. At least, I think he was."

"He was," Hopkins said confidently. "Why should Ledbetter find out that it was you?"

She reached for an answer but nothing came to mind. "Won't the Peelers—"

"My dear young lady, the Peelers will not be involved with that case. As soon as the magus is identified, the Royal Society will handle the investigation."

"That's even worse!" she said. "Why do you look so happy about it?"

"It's so refreshing, speaking to someone so innocent of how the world really works. My dear, nothing will come of it," Hopkins said. "As soon as Ledbetter's marks are identified, someone will ask him a couple of questions, he'll deny all involvement and then it will be forgotten. He'll make sure of it."

Charlotte was horrified. "But people have died! And what about the people murdered in that cage?"

Hopkins shrugged. "Heart failure is a tragedy no one can prevent."

Her fists balled tight. "But that's so wrong! What's to stop him recruiting others to use that cage?"

"What indeed," Hopkins said, pulling off his second glove. He tilted his head, examining her. "You really are furious about this, aren't you?"

The question confused her. "How can I not be, sir?"

He seemed to be delighted by her. "Indeed. Now, before I move on to more pressing matters, I want to reassure you that your father is no longer at risk."

"I know, I—" She stopped herself, reddening again. How she wished she could stop herself doing that!

"You doctored the paperwork, yes, I know. A rather clumsy attempt, but impressive, considering what you had just experienced. I've tidied up the loose ends you left in the paper trail, and he will receive a letter by second post, informing him that the debt has been repaid by an anonymous benefactor. The others who owed money will receive the same letter."

Charlotte had no idea how to feel. Grateful? Relieved? Happy? She should feel any and all of those, but all she felt was a growing suspicion that Hopkins knew far more about what she'd been doing over the past two nights than he was letting on. He had dropped hints, given her enough information to act but not see the whole picture, commented on her performance as if... "This was a test!"

His smile was divine and she had to consciously stop herself from reciprocating it. "At last, the Latent sees beyond the end of her own nose!"

"Don't call me that."

"Why ever not? That's what you are. As soon as Ainsworth told me about the candle, I suspected it. Your brother just wasn't confident enough, and you . . ." He trailed off, looking deep into her eyes for a moment. "You were so clearly trying to hide the sun behind a paper fan."

It felt like the tiniest bolt of lightning sparked through her breast.

"When I saw the way you peeped at the clock when that boy distracted everyone during Ben's test, I knew I was right. I went upstairs, saw your room was above, poked around, found a loose floorboard above the ceiling rose and then"—he patted the sketchbook resting on the seat next to him—"this simply confirmed my suspicions. You made the first timepiece change, didn't you? But your father assumed it was your brother and somehow you persuaded him to test instead of you. I can only assume he has some small ability—otherwise, it would have been madness to even try. That's why you asked about a drop in ability after testing, that time in the kitchen. Your questions made so much more sense when I put it together."

He seemed happy rather than accusatory, and her fear

that he was about to expose her faded a little. But she still couldn't bring herself to admit he was right.

Hopkins leaned forward, a bright excitement in his eyes that sent another thrill through her. "Miss Gunn, there's no need to be afraid; you are exactly what I've been looking for all this time. Someone who has more than just a shred of decency, who actually cares about people."

"Unlike you!" she said, trying to fight against the pull of his enthusiasm.

"On the contrary, Miss Gunn, I care a great deal about people. I simply choose to hide the fact to protect myself. Something you know all about, I fancy. How you have managed to hide your ability all this time astounds me. And not only that, but a career as an illustrator, too. It's quite remarkable what people are able to overlook."

Of course; some of her preliminary sketches for the poetry book were in the same sketchbook. He had discovered everything she had worked so hard to hide. She let her head flop back and covered her face. She was so tired and her head ached and she had felt so many emotions over the past twenty-four hours that she never wanted to feel anything ever again. "I don't understand what you want from me, Magus Hopkins. It's clear there is something you desire, but forgive me, I haven't slept for two days and my mind is not at its sharpest. Are you planning to turn me over to the Enforcers? Is that where you're taking me? Because at this moment, I am too tired and confused and heartsore to care."

When she let her hands drop into her lap, he took one and held it gently between both of his. "No, Miss Gunn. I'm not going to report you and I'm not going to urge you to submit yourself, either. But soon you will turn wild and you will be a great danger to yourself and others, unless . . ." He held her hand more firmly, passionately, almost. "Unless you agree to let me help you. Without the knowledge of the Royal Society."

Charlotte wanted to pull away as much as she wanted to kiss him, and neither seemed at all permissible. He was so much more forward than a gentleman had any right to be, and yet a part of her gloried at his touch, whilst another part berated her for her betrayal.

"You're willing to help me to break the law? You're a Fellow of the Royal Society!"

Hopkins nodded. "It's clear you don't want to lose what you have. You love a man and want to marry and, presumably, continue your career as an illustrator. Becoming a Fellow of the Royal Society would make both impossible, just as surely as it would teach you to control your power before it becomes too destructive." He edged even closer to her, so their knees were almost touching. It felt wildly inappropriate but she simply couldn't move.

"Just as surely as it would harness you, like a yoke on an ox. The Royal Society offers knowledge and protection at the price of freedom. Miss Gunn, I want you to keep your freedom *and* learn control. I can give you both."

"I suspect you aren't offering this to me so I can be a happily married woman."

"It isn't entirely altruistic, I'll grant you that. This business with the cage . . . it's only one of many atrocities being committed by the Royal Society, and I am literally powerless to act, to even investigate many of them. I need someone whom I can trust, someone with esoteric knowledge and skill, but also the freedom to go places and speak to people I cannot. I will teach you how to focus, how to direct your power and keep control of it, without informing the Royal Society of your ability. In return, I want you to help me investigate the crimes I know are being committed, and bring those responsible to justice."

She closed her eyes, trying to shut out the noise of his beauty so she could think. His hands were warm and soft, not those of a working man at all. He smelt of vanilla and something musky that made her want to close the gap between them so she could breathe it in more deeply.

In the darkness, rocked by the carriage, the sounds of London dull against the clatter of the horses' hooves and the rumble of the wheels on the cobblestones, Charlotte could feel the shape of the choices ahead of her. She could say no, but what then? Would he keep her ability a secret if she was soon to turn wild and endanger others? Unlikely. But if she accepted, what dangers would he lead her into? Crimes committed by the Royal Society were never going to be safe to investigate. And she would see more of him, share a dangerous secret with him, and surely that would bring them closer together? How could she want that so badly and yet need to run from it as far as she could?

But if he was telling the truth, this was her chance to make a difference. Her chance to retain some sort of freedom, despite the power that grew within her, to forge a life of her own.

No. It wasn't as simple as that.

Keeping her eyes closed, she said, "You speak of bringing those responsible to justice, but you didn't act against Ledbetter."

"It isn't the right time. A man as powerful and as wealthy as him can't be stopped easily."

That made sense. But even if she let that go, there was something that he couldn't deny. "You say that you'll help me, teach me what I need to know and not tell the Royal Society."

"If you agree to this, I will give you my word that I will never report you, and if it's in my power to do so, I will stop others from doing the same." His voice was so rich, so soft.

"But I wouldn't be free, would I?" She opened her eyes, forcing herself to look into his. "I would be yours. So to speak."

He said nothing for the longest moment, and she felt as if something were pulling her towards him that she had to actively resist. "Yes, Miss Gunn," he finally said. "I suppose you would be mine. My student, that is. And my assistant. My eyes and ears, from time to time."

"And it would be dangerous. From time to time?"

"I think the likelihood of that is rather high, Miss Gunn." His eyes flicked to her lips and then back up again. "Frightfully so, if truth be told. But I have the suspicion that a young lady as bright and able as you might actually enjoy that."

"I fear I have no choice but to accept, Magus Hopkins."

His eyes sparkled. "Together, we will work wonders, Miss Gunn." He glanced out of the window. "Ah, we're almost there."

"Where?"

"Your house, of course!" He laughed. "It was a very scenic route."

She looked out at a suddenly familiar street. "When do we begin, Magus?"

"I will send word when I've made arrangements. For

now, rest, spend time with your family and your fiancé. There's a possibility you will need to travel soon and I need you to be ready for adventure." He kissed her hand and gave her the sketchbook. "I will never steal from you again."

"Then I will never curse your name and call you despicable again."

He gave a nod, satisfied. "Good day to you, then, Miss Gunn. I will be in touch."

Once she was out of the carriage at the end of the street, watching it speed off, Charlotte struggled to believe the conversation had even happened. She looked down at the sketchbook and flipped through the pages until she came to her drawings of the timepiece. How strange to think that just these little drawings had done so much to change their lives. Then she noticed the slip of paper tucked into folds of the page.

Should you ever need me, for whatever reason, post a drawing of a clockface showing five past midnight through the letterbox of the clock tower closest to your house. I will come as soon as I am able.

It was from Magus Hopkins, it had to be. He put it there before the conversation in the carriage. Was it a sign of his arrogance that he was so certain he'd be able to recruit her, or simply the prediction that her choices were so limited that she was bound to say yes?

"Charlotte!"

The sound of George's voice calling her name made her spin around. She had completely forgotten he was coming to take her out for the afternoon. He was striding towards her, his hair shining in the winter sunshine, a broad smile on his face at the sight of her. She slapped the sketchbook shut, crumpling the note in her fist as she ran over. He kissed her on the cheek, cupping her face with his hand, tenderly.

"Hello, darling," he said. "Gosh, but you do look lovely today, Charlotte. What's put such a glow in your cheeks?"

Charlotte slipped her arm through his and they fell into step easily. "Let me drop this off at home and I will tell you all about it," she lied.

"What's that you have there?"

Perhaps it was time to tell him about her illustrations, especially as there was so much she wouldn't be able to share with him. "A sketchbook."

"Oh, for your father. Splendid!"

Charlotte couldn't find it in herself to correct him. She'd been hiding that part of herself for so long now, it felt false to speak of it. She slipped the note into the pocket of her coat as they walked, trying hard not to think about how Magus Hopkins had seen through all her deception to catch sight of who she really was. "I have so much to tell you, George," she said, forcing her mind to her fiancé. "You simply wouldn't believe everything that has happened since I last saw you!"

Acknowledgments

Thanks first and foremost to Lee Harris, my editor, who has been an excellent friend and given good advice throughout the ups and downs of my career to date. It's great to be working with you again, Lee!

Thanks to my agent, Jennifer Udden of the Barry Goldblatt Literary Agency, for sanity checks and edits.

And, of course, thanks always to Peter. For everything.

About the Author

Photograph by Lou Abercrombie

EMMA NEWMAN writes dark short stories and science fiction and urban fantasy novels. She won the British Fantasy Best Short Story Award 2015, and *Between Two Thorns,* the first book in Emma's Split Worlds urban fantasy series, was short-listed for the British Fantasy Best Novel and Best Newcomer 2014 awards. Her first science fiction novel, *Planetfall,* was published by Roc in 2015. Emma is an audiobook narrator and also cowrites and hosts the Hugo-nominated, Alfie Award–winning podcast *Tea and Jeopardy*. Her hobbies include dressmaking and playing RPGs. She blogs at www.enewman.co.uk and can be found as @emapocalyptic on Twitter.

TOR · COM

Science fiction. Fantasy. The universe. And related subjects.

*

More than just a publisher's website, *Tor.com* is a venue for **original fiction, comics,** and **discussion** of the entire field of SF and fantasy, in all media and from all sources. Visit our site today — and join the conversation yourself.

CPSIA information can be obtained
at www.ICGtesting.com
Printed in the USA
LVOW12s1923210917
549568LV00001B/3/P